Robbie O'Grady

A
SEQUENCE
OF EVENTS

Bloomington, IN Milton Keynes, UK

authorHOUSE®

AuthorHouse™
1663 Liberty Drive, Suite 200
Bloomington, IN 47403
www.authorhouse.com
Phone: 1-800-839-8640

AuthorHouse™ UK Ltd.
500 Avebury Boulevard
Central Milton Keynes, MK9 2BE
www.authorhouse.co.uk
Phone: 08001974150

First published by AuthorHouse 9/18/2006

ISBN: 1-4259-4907-X (sc)

Printed in the United States of America
Bloomington, Indiana

This book is printed on acid-free paper.

Radio Astronomy, Hemlock

Heavy Fuel Flu.

I travelled the years to find him there.
And was greeted by the spell of his merciless glare.
I begged him 'Please' to wait a while.
But was refused through the heat of his ice cold smile.

(Anonymous)

PROLOGUE

Have you ever met someone you thought to be a bit of a yarn spinner but they told the story so well that you couldn't be sure?

Maybe you have been on holiday and you have asked a fellow holiday maker what they did for a living and they have said "Well I'm a professional footballer, I play for Chelsea reserves, I have had a place in the first team but I'm injured at the moment and cant play." If you didn't know your football what else would stop you believing them?

What about the guy who doesn't say anything in particular he just hides his face when he gets caught in a camera shot, making out like he is some sort of celebrity who won't be photographed for free? There are plenty of these people about and usually you just know they are lying through their teeth to you. I always thought I would be pretty good at catching out one of them if I ever found myself in their company, and many times I have. To avoid confrontation we usually just agree and let them babble on, then when we get home tell our partner all about the lottery winner we just met on the train, who was travelling by train because his Porsche had just broke down and they had no courtesy cars left. Some times though their very appearance tells you they are genuine. Or leads you to believe they are.

On travelling home from a holiday in Florida I met Malcolm Wilson. In his late thirties he was a pretty ordinary looking bloke. Quite thick set and well weathered. His Scouse accent to the air stewardess was the ice breaker for the long flight ahead. Having spent the first fourteen years of my life living a stones throw from where he had been brought up some years previous, we began talking schools and names of roads. He asked what I did and I asked him 'for a living or for fun'? I told him my job was pretty boring but in my spare time I had been writing some articles on various tourist destinations and was trying to persuade certain tourism agencies to buy them from me.

"So you like to write?" He asked.

A couple of hours into the flight, after the general chit chat had turned into real conversation he asked me if I would consider putting *his* story on paper. I joked about it for a while not taking him the least bit serious and bombarding him with questions. What would it be about? Is it a real story? How long would it be? Because I'm hoping to get a couple of hours sleep in before we land.

"Its not one I could tell you all today, it would take a couple months at least." He said.

I was unsure, to be honest I couldn't even take him seriously. He assured me it would be enjoyable for me to write but of course there would be some conditions attached.

Firstly he wouldn't confirm whether any of it was true until I'd finished writing it for him. Secondly I had to promise that I wouldn't share it with anyone else. Lastly if he broke his word to me during the course of the job he would hold no grudges if I broke my word to him. He would pay me by day providing I didn't take longer than six months and a bonus at the end for a typed copy.

I really didn't know what to make of it. I fancied the challenge but what if he was having me on? The job I was doing was nothing special; I could find something similar at the drop of a hat but all that messing round. Was it worth it?

For reasons known only to myself I took the job. I spent the next few months travelling to his very tasteful detached house in West Derby making notes and compiling the following.

Make your own mind up.

CHAPTER 1

Being sixteen in 1983 was probably the best time to be sixteen. The eighties was, as well as being its own era, a transitional period from the 'behind the times' seventies to the futuristic sounding nineties. Music had reached a new level, CD players and microwaves were the latest must haves and a lot of Britons had been left with a remarkable sense of pride and respect for the heroic and courageous efforts of its Armed forces during the Falklands conflict and the Iranian embassy siege. The fact that the unemployment rate was well over three million meant nothing to me. Three years ago I was thirteen and totally clueless as to what I wanted to be after school, until I watched a gang of men in black smash through windows into a burning building and shoot a load of bad guys. Two years after that the Prime Minister sent hundreds more to a small group of islands called the Falklands, which I thought was up in Scotland to sort out another bunch of 'bad guys' for attempting to take what belonged to us. That was it for me, at almost seventeen I loved Britain and hadn't even considered doing anything else with my life other than fighting for it.

I left for the Army Training Regiment in Scotland from Liverpool Lime Street. It was a Tuesday morning, bitterly cold and I was alone, no friends or family to wish me well and the dark skies and drizzle were emphasising the fact that my life was not going to get much better over the next six months. I knew how much I wanted to be a soldier but never the less fear and doubt were setting in before the train even pulled off.

The train journey was long yet some how, not as long as I wished it to be. Each station the train arrived at brought me that much closer to a destination that I was still unsure I should be at. I found myself willing the train to slow down or even turn back for a few days, just until I could be sure of my decision. At seventeen the next six months should include borrowing Dad's car, parking up in the CoOp car park until two in the morning, bottles of cider and girls on the back seat. I was headed for a life a world away from this and staring out of the window of that train was I only then starting to realise that the life of a soldier was a far cry from that which had been promised to me in the movies.

Although I was extremely anxious about my chosen profession at the same time I felt excitement and pride in myself for doing something a hell of a lot more meaningful than the lads I'd left back in the CoOp car park. It was just that the unease was much more powerful an emotion than the pride.

I was picked up at Edinburgh train station by a Corporal of my training team, there were about twenty to thirty other unsuspecting candidates who had got off various other trains and some were dropped off at the camp by their parents. No one was over twenty, all naive kids who thought they were cooler and harder than each other, including myself. Too many of us thought the whole thing was going to be easier than it actually was. What is it about teenagers that make them believe that they know better? Why do they convince themselves that no one has been there before them and even if they had they were going to do so much better than them? The Army has got to be the best place for a teenager because training depot Full Screws hate the spotty fuckers and it doesn't take them long to knock that arrogant streak out of them. Literally.

If I was asked to explain the training manifesto of the British Army without talking too much shit and boring the inquisitor I would describe it in two parts. The 'Breaking' and the 'Making'. For an instructor to successfully train a body of men to the same standard all candidates must be a clean slate and of the same frame of mind. The best way to do this is to take them to the lowest point of their lives, together. Break them, run them into the ground until they cant breathe then run them twice the distance again. Starve them in the pissing rain for four days with nothing but a boil-in-the-bag casserole and some dry biscuits to eat. Take them to a place they would cut a finger off not to be and take them there together. Of course none of this goes on in the British Army. The training teams have tough but achievable targets to set the candidates and they stick to them. I imagined most of the torture. Honest.

At this low point you will achieve two very important requirements. You will extract the weak from the group, the ones who do not belong there. Regardless of what any human rights group tells you an Infantry unit is no place for anyone with sub standard values and weakness is one of these.

Secondly you will achieve unity, the group members will learn that looking after number one will not work anymore. With all your personal effects taken away and with no where to go on your own you will learn that doing for each other brings greater benefits than doing for yourself. The instructors will also introduce communal punishment. One of you fucks up and you all get the beasting. Persistent offenders are then punished within the group causing them to either leave or mend their ways. Don't worry this isn't a guide book for training a soldier, I'm just painting a picture. Bear with me.

The punishment given out by the group is probably sixty percent retribution as the members will feel hard done to that they were punished for something they didn't do. It's near impossible to see the benefits of communal punishment when you are first introduced to it. The remaining forty percent is probably genuine preventative maintenance. In all honesty, its no fun giving a weaker team member a beating when its guaranteed he's feeling just as shit as you are and a whole lot shittier after he's been briefed, but I didn't see it fail, they either leave or wise up.

The corrective punishment administered by the group to its own members is by no means to be confused with bullying. Bullies do what they do for personal reasons, usually to make themselves feel more powerful. As much as those who remain victims by not confronting their oppressors do not belong in this group, I didn't personally consider bullying to be an efficient method of removal, not because I was sympathetic towards the victims, I didn't give a shit, but because it was being carried out for personal gain and the group as a whole achieved nothing from it.

In one instance I found myself in the washrooms interrupting a weaker member being throttled by someone who could only be described as a gorilla. His prey was arched over backwards with the back of his head in the sink. There was blood around the area, which we later found to be from a cut at the back of his ear which he had received as his head had been rammed into the sink and the edge of the metal tap had found its way into the flesh covering the bony lump of skull behind his ear. His face was bright red and stained from tears which made it clear to me that this particular episode had been going on for quite a few minutes. He was only a slight lad, in all honesty he had no place in an Infantry Regiment. At a guess I would say he had been in cadets since being at school and had made a grave mistake in thinking the life of camping out and playing hide and seek in combat gear would continue in the Army. I had no sympathy for him at all, in fact he made me angry. I was beginning to pride myself on the fact that I was handling the training well and slowly but surely I was becoming the soldier I had set out to be. I was also proud of most of my platoon. We all looked good out on the ranges and forced marches and were fearsome and intimidating as a group. He was letting the side down, he didn't look the part couldn't keep up on runs and couldn't hit a barn door from ten feet with his personal weapon. He did not belong here.

However, what was going on here was over and above what was needed to phase him out. His attacker was enjoying his role, laughing at him and belittling him as much as possible. He wasn't doing it for the platoon, he was doing this for himself. He had no place here just as much as the lad he had held of. Two people at two opposite ends of a scale that did not belong in my life or the life of the rest of the lads. Being that I was the only one in the room that, in my opinion did belong here I felt that the responsibility somehow fell on me to do something to end this ordeal. Plus I'd be the first one to get some fight credits, for as I remember this was the first fight in my platoon and there would be quite a few credits on offer for this big fucker.

I walked over smiling, making out that I agreed with what was going on and would either join in at some point or just turn a blind eye. He said something about him being a fag and a useless twat then asked me what I thought. He had his back to me and before he had chance to ask me a second time I had put the steel mop bucket over the back of his head. It didn't put him down but I'll bet my house it hurt. He turned round fast to do something about it but I didn't give him any thinking time at all and before it had even registered that it was the mop bucket that had just split the back of his head open I had dropped it and my right fist was on its way up to his chin at mach two. That put the fucker down.

There was some shouting and screaming after that but it mostly involved him screaming and me shouting while I stamped on him a few times. I stopped momentarily while I asked the weakling to take advantage of his attacker's now less dominant position, and unleash his nemesis. He gave me a half smile then muttered some shit about not wanting to lower himself to his level. I told him to fuck off then after he'd left I gave the 'you're as bad as him' speech to the lump of sorry lard lying on the previously spotless washroom floor.

When I returned to my bed space the weakling was waiting to thank me, I didn't think it would be worth trying to explain to him that I didn't do it for him so I just told him to go away in the most impolite way possible, the last thing I needed at this tough time was this no hoper thinking he'd made a friend he could latch onto for the next five months.

The incident was covered up, I had an idea it would be even though I had only known the rest of the lads for a matter of weeks. No cover story is more water tight than that of an Infantry platoon believe me. By this point we'd had a code installed into us that cannot be learnt or taught it just develops under the circumstances. You start to feel that you would only be doing yourself an injustice by dropping your mucker in it, so you do your best to cover for him and don't crack or slip up whatever it takes. "Loyalty above all but Honour" or something like that. Since it would be dishonourable to be disloyal its kind of a catch twenty two. If you know what I mean.

It was while lay in my bed that night that I discovered how dangerous a persons conscience could be, especially to an Infantryman. What if I had of taken him under my wing? I'd have been doing the work of two people for the duration of my training. Then, if by some miracle he did make it through training the country would have had someone on their front line that couldn't even bring himself to harm a man who had physically and mentally tortured him for that ten minutes in the washrooms. How could he ever bring himself to drive a cold hard bayonet into the stomach of someone he had never met? I didn't feel the slightest bit guilty. I did however come to realise it wasn't him I hated, I'm sure he was a really nice guy and was no doubt very good at something, just not being a soldier. I hated him being here that was all. All the other weaklings had realised there place and left by this point, why was he still here?

He lasted another week or so after that. I could almost respect his determination, but if he had have been honest with himself he would have realised he was trying to flog a dead horse, there was no hope. By week seven he had gone and the rest of us were left to complete the first eleven weeks unhindered.

My basic and phase one training taught me an awful lot of soldiering skills. I always said during conflicts that if we could have a hard drive fitted into our heads that allowed us to call up the required aspect of training on demand and carry it out flawlessly we'd be fuckin invincible. I mean don't get me wrong the British are one of the best at doing this but you try reciting and executing the marksmanship principles before every shot when your getting it from six different positions. "The weapon must point naturally at the target, without any undue physical effort." I don't fuckin think so.

By the time my Passing out parade came I was itching to get to my Battalion. Most of my platoon loved the day. Their parents had made the long trek up to Scotland to watch 'mummy's little soldier' showing off their skills on the assault course, followed by a stroll over to Lé Cookhouse to sample culinary delights of the Catering Corps. Meanwhile we all went to get changed into our number two's so we could march around the square for two hours in the pissing rain.

I hated the day. Thinking about it now I suppose I was slightly bitter that no one was there to see me now I was the big tough soldier. My parents had emigrated to New Zealand just two weeks before I left for Scotland. After

I turned fifteen they lost interest in me. When I told my dad I had signed up his reply was "Oh that'll be fun for you." In the days that followed I convinced myself that he didn't believe I had it in me, or that I would bottle it and beg them to let me go to New Zealand with them. Their leaving date came and passed though and they left with a few tears and some good luck wishes for me. I didn't know this then but it would be eight years until I would see them again.

I stayed at some friend's houses for the next couple of weeks, getting pissed and basically just saying goodbye to the ordinary life I had become very bored of. My Passing out parade, I suppose, was another turning point in my young life. I had learnt all they had to teach me at the moment, now I wanted to use it. Get me off this drill square and give me my posting. I was gagging for it.

Nothing to get too excited over however! As I joined my regiment as they had just gotten settled in Tidworth on Salisbury plain. Burghport Barracks. What a shit hole. The only thing good about it was the fact that the post code was considered low risk by insurance companies and for those who had cars it kept their premiums down. Since I didn't have a car there was nothing good about it.

All was not lost though. Northern Ireland was very busy in the eighties and Companies from my Battalion were regularly being sent out there on six month tours. I was only in Tidworth three months and my name came up on Company detail to report to Battalion headquarters to get signed up for my Northern Ireland training.

Without violating the Official Secrets act too much Northern Ireland training was fuckin marvellous. It involved a lot of throwing wooden blocks and potatoes at each other in mock riots which nine times out of ten would turn out to be worse than the real ones in West Belfast. Lots of cuts and bruises to show for it, as well as another encyclopaedia of tactics and skills to save to my hard drive. My Brick Commander had this phrase. His timing in reciting it was always Impeccable usually when you had just been hit in the face with a block or were about to drift into a hypothermic comma on the 3am drag stag. He wouldn't wait until the pain had died off a little or give you a minute to recover, he would get you right at the point when the unbearable sensation was at its peak and you would do anything to be wrapped in cotton wool. He would put his big sausage fingered hand on your shoulder and say; "Don't worry about it lad, its all character building stuff."

CHAPTER 2

Nervous was not the word for my first tour. We arrived at Aldergrove sometime mid-morning in June 1984 . It was a sunny morning, which was good news. I don't know how I would have felt if it was dark and miserable again. I already had that one on the day I left for Scotland. I didn't need it now while the thought of being blown up with a pipe bomb or having my head taken off by a sniper was pinnacle in my mind. Funny how a bit of sunshine can keep a persons spirit up.

Everything moved really fast over here, I liked that. No hanging around waiting for transport. We couldn't afford to because of the current security status of the place. Stay in one spot too long and brutal exit was almost guaranteed. The security at the airports when we arrived was a lot tighter than it usually would be, not for my benefit of course but it made me feel better that as well as looking after the arrival of our motley crew the security forces had Ronald Reagan to think about.

The then President of the United States had just begun a four day visit to the Republic of Ireland to meet with the Dáil and Senate in Dublin, where he was to tell them that it was not US policy to interfere in matters relating to Northern Ireland. This may have been a good few miles south of where we were and not to mention in a different country but it didn't stop the Ray ban clad Secret Service covering every major facility on the entire island.

With regards to Presidents Reagan's comment on Ulster's situation, although I had briefly glanced over the politics behind the campaign I was only eighteen and back then I thought it wise to let my superiors deal with the formalities so I could concentrate on being a good soldier and do my bit for the bigger picture. I was a very small cog in a very big machine and although I contributed to the running of things, at this time I could be replaced quite easily so I kept my head down.

Of course they made attempts to educate us but I always managed to keep in the back of my mind that anything they tried to sell me was one-sided and although I would never talk about it, they were never going to convince me that it wasn't six of one and half a dozen of the other. My opinion wouldn't matter or change anything anyway. The only thing it would do is draw negative attention from my fellow soldiers. So I kept quiet and took a side. "A good soldier follows orders in an instant without hesitancy or question". Since that's all I wanted to be my views never came into it.

For the next three years I walked the fields and streets of Fermanagh, Tyrone Armagh and County Down, with the odd stint up in Londonderry and Antrim. I felt as though there wasn't an inch of ground in the whole of Northern Ireland my feet hadn't covered. Stories of riots and house searches are books in themselves. The importance of my time here was what it taught me. By 1987 I was more aware than a three headed cat. I was a Lance Jack with zero tolerance for halfwits. The Section Commander was similar so naturally the rest of the lads followed suit. Our contributions to the positive recognition of the Battalion did not go unmissed and our section was frequently mentioned when the Regiment received commendations.

My weapon drills were flawless. In 1985 the SA80 (Small Arms for the 80's) was introduced into service and by 1987 I could strip and rebuild it in less than sixty seconds in a pitch black room while Slash and Axl screamed Welcome To The Jungle into my ears at two thousand decibels. Yes I know, but they were long nights.

I never failed to score over sixty five out of seventy on my Annual Personal Weapons Test (APWT) and when they amended the test to allow for the SA80's greater accuracy I amended my score. I lived for this life. I loved every minute of it and with each day came new knowledge and new tasks. I took each day as it came, I carried out whatever task they gave me, the best way I knew how. I was oblivious to the fact someone much higher up the food chain had their eye on me.

I continued with this role with an ambition for promotion. 1988 brought me training in Jungle Warfare and '89 a trip to Norway for some Artic Warfare. The new decade brought with it a new war, the gulf, and despite my now extensive and exemplary military record I was not to visit this part of the world. Instead, on the 6th of December 1990, five months after the beginning of the Kuwait crisis I was asked to report to the OC's office for some news that would again send my life off in an entirely different direction.

My Company Commander was a short man, not much over five foot or so. As fit as they came and hard as nails. I considered my personal fitness to be way above average but when the Major joined us on a run I would cringe with shame as I struggled to stand up straight after it while he calmly smoked a B&H shaking his head at us. He spent most of his childhood in South Africa, his parents owned a vineyard over there and I can only assume he didn't see himself crushing grapes for a living so fled to Blighty to pursue a military career. Lucky for me he did. He liked hard workers and despite his hard hearted appearance he could never quite manage to hide the pride he felt in his men when they did well. That's how I knew I wasn't here for a bollocking. I could see pride in his face. There wasn't a glimmer of a smile and his body language gave nothing away, it was his eyes that told me something good was to come of this frosty Wednesday morning.

As hard as I try I can never remember his speech word for word. I understand that I should being that it was such an important milestone in my life but the exact words he used that day always seem to escape me. He had a gift of stringing sentences together that could deliver to your heart whatever emotion he required you to be feeling at that particular moment. If we had failed to achieve a certain time in our Basic Fitness Test he could make us feel like complete failures and if our drill was especially good one day we would feel as proud as punch with a single sentence. The special for today was 'awe'. About four sentences in, when he began telling me that someone outside the regiment had been monitoring my progress through Northern Ireland I convinced myself that it was the SAS. I was being asked if I would like to apply for selection. In all honesty, I shit my pants. I didn't know what to think or what I was going to say when he made the opportunity to speak available to me. However he was much cleverer than that. He knew that's exactly what I was thinking and to save me making a fool of myself he denied me of such an opportunity until he had made sure that I fully understood who the interested party was.

It is far from a common occurrence that Intelligence branches of the Armed Forces should contact an Infantry Regiment to request the services of its members. Should they require such skills they have Marines Para's and SAS at their disposal. During my tours of Northern Ireland I spent some time working along side the Joint Surveillance Groups (JSG) and Tactical Support Groups (TSG) in the Close Observation Platoon (COP). Duties usually included long stags in observation posts and tracking movements and habits of known and suspected players. Mostly all the jobs that need doing in the intelligence trade but the ones that the real spooks don't want to do. I always endeavoured to get back to my own platoon though because I always found that members of COP were slightly above their station. The fact that they received a clothing allowance to buy civvie clothes and were allowed to grow their hair to look less like Squaddies tended to lead them into the belief that they were Special Forces. So much so that some of them even stopped socialising with the rest of the Battalion to make themselves appear more covert. It just embarrassed me. You would hear people calling them allsorts in the NAAFI and rightly so, they were as much Special Forces as I was a 34 DD.

So why me? What exactly was going on here? The only time I could think of that any intelligence division would have noticed me was during my time in COP and I really hadn't done anything that special for them. I started thinking all sorts of possibilities some of which included words like 'expendable' 'scapegoat' and 'who gives a fuck about some Regular Army grunt'. I can only assume that this paranoia came from the fact that this was real and the only time I'd ever heard of shit like this was in the movies. My whole body was ice, like the feeling you get when you give blood having had nothing to eat and your blood sugar is so low that you blackout. I just wasn't blacking out, I thought I would at any moment but the Major's speech was so engrossing my brain wouldn't let me. What he went on to tell me brought me down a peg or two but the first five minutes, when I heard my name and Army Intelligence mentioned in the same sentence, kind of knocked me sideways. It turns out that whilst on one of my many Vehicle Checkpoint (VCP) duties just outside Lisnaskea, Co. Fermanagh, something happened that had a significant effect on an ongoing operation that until that day had come to a grinding halt.

Our Section's method of conducting a VCP was not strictly by the book but its important for me to describe the setting so it can be understood why I made the decision I made.

The VCP was made up of eight men and a Land Rover. The Section Commander remained within arms length of the Lanny, which we kept running and was off the main drag. One man would stop the traffic about fifteen to twenty meters away from me and another who would call the vehicles through as we saw fit and either let them pass unstopped or check them out. The remaining four would be posted two either end of the VCP about twenty to thirty meters away from myself depending on the area, never out of sight. The man with myself would cover me as I took the registration number and the names of the driver and passengers and radioed back to the OP's room where the duty signaller would run the checks on his Vengeful terminal and relay them back to me. So that's how it worked.

This particular day was the same as any other, stop vehicles run checks and either let them go or call over the attached RUC officer to take it further. The car that made the difference crawled up to the checkpoint as they all do and stopped at the first man. I sent the last car on its way and called the next up. As it crept towards me I locked eyes for the briefest of moments with the front seat passenger. I knew him. As soon as I realised I did I looked away and tried my hardest to look as though I didn't. I

20

had to stop this car now so I could reassure myself that it was who I thought it was. However if I did stop the car there was a very good chance that he might panic and cause myself and my seven colleagues to fall out with him. Too late, I'd stopped him. While I was deciding what to do my left arm had made its own way up into the air. I looked in and greeted them, three in total one in the middle of the back seat and two in the front. There was no friendly reply as such just an acknowledgement, these guys hated me and everything I represented, I could almost smell the hate inside the car but hey I was the one with the gun and seven mates. 'Where ya off to lads'? I asked. 'Pub' was the reply. 'Not be drinkin and drivin I hope'. This brought a slight increase in volume. '*What the fuck's that got to do with you*'? That's where I thought I'd leave the banter, I was already brickin it I was surprised they couldn't smell it. I told them I was just going to run a quick check on the car. I knew this wouldn't raise any alarms. I'd just run the check ask the drivers name and if it didn't match the owner's ask him why and accept whatever answer he gave me. As soon as they were on their way again I'd let the Ops room know that someone from our most wanted board had just passed through my VCP. This was my only option, I couldn't get the rest of my team involved now without the player knowing I knew him. Plus if there was any sort of surveillance Op going on I'd blow that too, besides there was very few roads they could turn onto in the time it would take me to let the OP's room know what was going on. Best decision I thought, let him through.

The most wanted board was a pin board full of photos of players that sightings of which needed to be reported immediately because their whereabouts was vital to the bigger picture. The board was just outside the Ops room and the rules where you had a good look at it before you went out on any patrols or VCP's, although no one ever did. I'd looked over it the odd time in passing.

So why the interest then? What was so special about a grunt doing what he was paid to do? Well the picture on the most wanted board was of a clean shaven man with cropped hair, proper ratty lookin' fucker. The man in the car however was a lot chubbier with a big curly black mop of hair and a beard to match. He had been in the States for four years arranging various arms deals and three years or so prior to today the powers that be had lost him in a French Cheese Fare in Boston. He hadn't been seen or heard of since and the fact that I spotted him in a moving car in Lisnaskea looking totally different than he did when he had his picture taken certainly stuck in someone's mind.

I had a knack for remembering things. Some of the lads reckoned I had a photographic memory but, I just had a knack for remembering things. I could remember vehicle registration numbers and the corresponding registered keeper details for months on end. Many times I had shocked civilians and the other lads by reeling off their details to them at VCP's without touching my radio. It was something I didn't have to try to do; the facts and figures just found a little spot in my brain and made themselves comfy for the next few months. Same with faces. Forget the few months, I never forgot a face. If I met you the next time I saw you, be it a week or ten years I'd remember you, and your name. Have all the plastic surgery you like, if you kept your eyes I'd remember you. I'd never really thought much of my ability until that day in the OC's office.

I agreed to the transfer. Of course I did. If I didn't like it they would always have me back here and who knew what new skills I'd bring back with me.

The next few months however I found myself thinking I'd made the biggest mistake ever. The courses I had to undertake to change my cap badge were to say the least more boring than the bits of Big Brother they show on E4 at 3am when all the sad plastic celebrities are asleep and the highlight is when one gets up for a piss. No I don't watch it.

The lectures were long and tiresome and the soggy fields of CrossMaglenn were looking more like Paradise every day. I stuck with it though, mostly for the Majors sake. He hated quitters and he thought a lot of me, if I came back after the training period then fine he'd accept that, but to quit the course half way through would lose me a lot of points. Besides, its all character building stuff right!

CHAPTER 3

For the task I was assigned to there was no reason why I couldn't have kept my cap badge and just been attached to them. I would have been much more comfortable with this. After all every soldier has pride in his cap badge and the Regiment Squadron or Battery he belongs to. There is however something about an Infantryman that is a cut above the rest when it comes to Regimental pride. A number of factors contribute to this, the fact that Infantry Divisions are the oldest in the Armed Forces. Dating back to way beyond the time of Alexander the Great, Gengus Kaan and other historically significant military leaders such as these. The first battle ever fought will have been fought by Infantrymen of some description, however crude and although they may have lacked the training available today their camaraderie was earned with blood and matching it in the Archery or Signals divisions would have taken some doing. Being a part of this unique bond brings with it a feeling of pride that like the bond itself cannot be matched in any other Battery Squadron or Fleet, though such a statement could be considered biased.

With the exception of divisions such as Artillery, skills from most Army departments can be transferred to civilian life. Signals - Air traffic control, REME - Industry and Medics - Hospitals. I can't think of any trade that would require hordes of wild eyed warriors storming down the high street with bayonets attached screaming like mad men or in the same sense a Battery of Bombardiers sat three miles away firing high explosive anti-tank rounds into an industrial estate. These departments serve their purpose in the forces then find themselves following a totally different vocation when entering civilian life.

From this solitude is born the need for a family type unit that understands each others loneliness. Social outcasts that ease each others pain. Like the homeless or the heroin addicts. No one understands them except themselves, they stay together as a group and share their guilt, they know sleeping rough or sticking that needle in their arm is a hard place to get back from but doing it with a friend, believe it or not makes it more acceptable to them. Like the nineteen year old Private about to storm the Iraqi bunker, although it won't be on his mind at the time, when he stops the burning phosphorus covered nineteen year old enemy kicking and screaming by plunging his bayonet into his chest there is no coming back. The fact that his mucker is next to him frantically stabbing at another poor soul makes him feel better, if only for a while. The next time he is alone with his thoughts, unless he is a completely cold hearted fucker its almost guaranteed he will start thinking about what family the guy had and how they will react to the news of his death. Will one of them have to identify the body? Who will do it? How will they do it when his face is covered in slash marks from my bayonet? Did I have to kill him, could I not just have detained him? What if he had kids? After his first kill this Private Soldier, who isn't even old enough to buy alcohol in the States will ask himself all these questions and many more. I never met anyone who got a good nights sleep after their first kill.

Like everything in life though the killing gets easier, the questions get less and the good night's sleep becomes more achievable. After five or so you resign yourself to the fact that a leader, who has been voted in by millions of hard working decent citizens, has issued you an order to fight and kill the soldiers of a leader who has forced his way into leadership. The fact that his soldiers probably had no say in their chosen profession is irrelevant, you are a necessary evil, they are in the wrong place at the wrong time, if they do not die the enemy will win and millions more of innocent people will suffer because of it.

The government spends millions training these men to kill on instinct or word of command removing their emotions during training and turning them into ruthless killing machines, then when one of them goes off the rails in civilian life and murders someone the courts tell them that they exercised no control and should have channelled their energy in a more positive manor. As much as I would never expect any court to show leniency towards these victims this is what they are, victims. I would never presume either to know the solution to this catch twenty two situation. Lucky for me when I was force fed the taste for blood the powers that be kept it coming.

I'll not drone on about the months spent on training courses and in lecture theatres for two reasons, firstly I could quite possibly be in breach of the Official Secrets Act and secondly it would almost certainly bore you to death. Instead we'll go straight to my first assignment with Army Intelligence.

The 6th of July 1991, I was assigned to work along side a US Customs Official called Mike at Gatwick Airport. When I was first introduced to him he still smelt strongly of alcohol from his Independence Day celebrations two days previous in the bar of the Holiday Inn. He made sure I knew every detail of the night during our long chats whilst posing as airport security staff. He was a very thick set lad, loud and extremely gung ho. Just like something fresh out of Hollywood, sunglasses on dark days and a piece of gum constantly in his mouth.

As much as I make him out to be a typical John Wayne type American Fly boy who turned up pissed on the job this guy knew his stuff. He had ten years on me and his knowledge of the game and how to play couldn't be faulted. This guy had my respect from day one.

A typical day involved the two of us sat at passport inspection desks waiting for a glimpse of a player. Higher up the food chain they had Intel of a possible arrival of Palestinian arms dealer who was expected in London for a meeting with some of our old friends from Belfast. Naturally the details were kept from me, I always suspected Mike knew more than he let on but at this point I wasn't bothered, I was just enjoying being part of the team. As sad as it sounds I felt like James Bond and all I wanted was for this bird brain terrorist to turn up at my desk so I could I.D. him and get yet another pat on the back.

The fact that there are so many possible routes into the UK from the Middle East meant I spent most of my days running from one desk to another and even then there was no guarantee he was going to turn up on my shift, if indeed he was going to turn up at all.

The shifts were fourteen hours long and you ate drank and pissed in between flight arrivals. We had oppo's who worked the alternate shift who 'apparently' were just as good as us. It was nothing to write home about, long boring and when you sat and thought about it a fuckin' waste of time. After the first fortnight I settled into it and the excitement along with the James Bond feeling died off and the highlight of my day changed from unloading reloading and making safe my Browning in the Public toilets to talking about Mike's time in Cuba with the US Rangers.

At first his accent and the way he told his stories led me to believe this guy had watched one too many movies. Until now I had never talked about any of my jobs, unless someone asked me and even then I tried my hardest to tone it down as much as possible. I would always see myself in their position, thinking to themselves 'fuck me this guy's full of shit'. Although it should never have mattered to me what people thought I could never bare the fact that they might consider me a bullshitter.

I would only ever tell stories about my time in the Infantry. To me this was safe stuff to talk about. I would never discuss anything I did inside Army Intel even to others like me, I just felt safer with no one else knowing plus I would always be suspicious that anyone interested in hearing about me sat at a passport inspection desk for fourteen hours a day almost certainly had an ulterior motive.

I could quite happily sit for hours in the bar of the Gatwick Airport Holiday Inn though listening to Mike make a 3am stag in a Guantanamo Bay Sanger sound like a Hollywood blockbuster.

He had an authority over me that came not from rank but from the fact that he was ten years older and had done so much more. Rank never came into it, he took me under his wing and probably looked at me as much his apprentice as I did him my mentor. Ironic I suppose that I should join the Army to escape the mundane life of a days work and a night in the local, to go on to forge my most treasured friendship in a bar over a few pints after a days work anyway.

We both acted as a respite to each other after such long boring days and although I used to think that he'd done this for years and probably had mates like me all over the world, I later went on to learn that he was as lonely in the job as I was and the fact that he had done it for longer just made him lonelier, soon we'd both be on different assignments and the friendship we had forged over the countless two pound pints of Stella would, like the assignment itself, move on.

The sighting of the Palestinian lost its importance and never happened as did the next job and the next job, after four months I started thinking this was it, this was how I was to spend the rest of my days waiting for my pension to kick in. The nights in the bars lost their edge and it wasn't long before I lost mine. Lying in the perfectly made bed in my clinical Holiday Inn hotel room I found myself thinking I had made a mistake after all. I longed to be anywhere but here, the Gulf Bosnia anywhere but here. I was losing my soldiering skills, forgetting vital drills. The clean sheets felt wrong, I was a Grunt I needed my fart sack and bivvie bag and a brew at 4am heated in a mess tin on hexy blocks and sipped slowly from my Army issue black plastic mug. Rivalli at five to the sound of gunfire and running six miles before I'd even woke up. Time to tell the boss his little brain fart was over, I wasn't cut out to be a Spook.

Returning to my old Company was not to be as easy as I had hoped it would be. They had spent too much on me now and I already knew too much. It was easier for them to just ask me what it would take to reconsider my position. I told them how I missed being in the field and the daily thrill of having to be constantly alert to my environment. I missed being a soldier.

It just so happens, they told me, that Bosnia was quite exciting this time of year. How would I fancy a trip over there? 'Sign me up' I told them, 'When can I leave?'.

CHAPTER 4

After a couple of months hanging around in Reading and Bulford near Salisbury I was deployed to Bosnia with a handful of other Army Int Field Operatives. We landed at Split Airport in Croatia where the Logistics had the place set up really well. We stayed the night in Army bunks in a building being used for Military Freight storage. Emotions that night were similar to those of the night before I left for Scotland, this was after all the first place I had been to with anything going on outside of the UK. The only action I had seen was Northern Ireland. I was back at that place again, the unknown. I had been here enough times now however to be finding the 'unknown' familiar territory. I was starting to feel that I could be sent anywhere and handle it. I wont lie though and try and sell myself as the big tough hard man, as I remember I was very apprehensive about the whole situation, I had heard stories of mines in the footpaths and homemade vodka fuelled snipers in the hills. This was a totally different war to the one being fought in Ulster, here we didn't know who liked us and when. At least in Northern Ireland we knew everyone hated us.

Although I felt I was sufficiently time served by now I was still only twenty six. It had been noted how well I was doing and how much I had achieved for my age but all said and done I was still the 'Sprog', especially in the present company. Obviously they had a degree of respect for my time spent in Ireland and the fact that I was poached by the gaffer rather than transferring by my own request. Even so I was still the butt of the occasional joke, I didn't mind though I knew it came with the turf and I liked the fact that despite their backgrounds each one of them knew how far they could push me before I stopped seeing the funny side. We had been together as a group for a couple of months now and although it was still early days we all got on well and there were no personality clashes to create bad air.

The next morning, after a night of reminiscing amongst ourselves and getting to know each other. Sharing war stories and opinions on the various conflicts around the globe we took a ferry from Split to a small island off the coast called Brache. We stayed in a hotel where we had hired a conference room which we would visit every day for the next week and discuss exactly what our role here would involve. Basically what had caused the conflict how the United Nations thought they could fix it and what part we would be playing in it all.

The Rules of Engagement in the early Ninety's were almost non-existent. At one point all our soldiers could do was stand and watch as hundreds of innocent civilians were massacred. So in the months that followed any operations involving the aggressive discharging of any munitions usually had to remain as covert as possible.

Opinions of the cause of the conflict varied widely, depending on where in the country you were and who's opinion you asked. For reasons unknown to myself and my colleagues Western Press failed, or decided not to report on probably the majority of attacks carried out by two of the warring factions. In my opinion I would have to say that they had been instructed not to by a higher power. Instead, for reasons still beyond my comprehension an awful lot of suspect occurrences took place to enable the press to pin most of the blame on the Serbs. Of course I only heard the details of these incidents second hand so how true they were could also be questioned.

A couple of months previous on May 27ᵗʰ at around four o'clock, there was an attack known as "The Bread Line Massacre". This took place in the market place at Sarajevo. Innocent civilians queued up for bread from a local bakery when they were killed by an explosion which was alleged to be Muslim mortar fire. In all twenty two

people were killed. According to reports, most of these twenty two were Serbs. TV crews were already set up at this site to film other going's on and immediately filmed the carnage and broadcast it over and over around the world. At this point however it wasn't clear who carried out the attack and when a confidential report detailing the event reached the European reporters, the fact that the massacre was engineered by Muslims was reported by very few Western newspapers. Instead most Western media outlets, mainly TV stations used the massacre to blame the Serbs.

A few days after the Breadline Killings a report was written about the current situation in Bosnia which showed that the majority of carnage was being caused by Croats. This report went on to be stolen by an Austrian Official working in the UN. Although it was a three sided civil war it appeared to me that other world leaders were engineering it to be the Serbs fault, but what the fuck do I know. Although I was briefed on the political history of the place I again endeavoured to keep an open mind and base my opinion only on what I seen for myself. Like Northern Ireland I could never fully agree with either side and what would it matter if I could? I was not a politician, I was a Field Op here to do whatever my superiors asked of me in the hope that they had got it right and were moving towards a permanent solution. However if pressed for an answer of who was most to blame I would have to say the Serbs and the Croats, and the Muslims too.

Humour me while I take a moment to illustrate the type of war being fought. This wasn't soldiers hiding in trenches firing at one another, this was unlawful genocide and although I too have used the Serbs as examples make no mistake, the other groups were just as capable of the same carnage.

Under the command of Slovidan Milochovich the Serbian Generals would round up hundreds of Muslims at a time and order them to dig their own graves. On completion they would execute them, leaving five or six alive to bury the dead. When the dead were buried the remaining would be executed and buried by the Serbian soldiers. The women would be dragged from their homes kicking and screaming then raped and murdered in front of their children. After they had watched this many of the children would be raped and murdered too. The Serbian soldiers thought nothing of raping a Muslim or Croat man either, to them the word homosexual didn't come into it, it was emasculating for their enemy so they did it. These guys were animals and they loved the fact that the rest of the world thought so. The same however went for the Croats and the Muslims. Nothing about this conflict was black and white.

In my opinion there were several wars going on in Bosnia at the same time. The Russian Orthodox Serbs were fighting the Muslims, the Muslims were fighting back and in there somewhere were the Catholic Croatians. Again like all wars it was based around that trouble making fairytale 'Religion'.

Along with this three way war the United Nations were in there applying their own tactics in an attempt to enforce peace. The United Nations is made up of Armed Forces from a range of free world countries. Each one of these countries having a leader who probably has his or her own spin on the goings on in the 'Theatre' (the name given by serving UN and NATO forces to the Bosnian trouble zone).

The brain box's in MI6 and the CIA, on being given permission by their superiors who can then hide under the 'Plausible Denial' umbrella, would be 'allowed' to carry out certain operations which in their eyes would either draw the war to a close, make their own governments money or assist in the damage limitation program and earn them points from the UN, who also endeavoured to remain in a position where they could deny all knowledge.

Operations ranged from locating weapons dumps and destroying them to assassinating key military figures within the warring factions. Of course every effort was made to ensure that no one ever looked in the direction of the Western World when pointing the finger of blame. The fact that there were so many different warring factions meant we were never short of someone to blame.

In August 92 I was holding up in the town of Vitez, about sixty or so kilometres outside Sarajevo carrying out basic Intel Ops, tracking munitions movements via satellite imagery and putting reports together from info gathered from the regulars whilst on their endless patrols. Occasionally I'd tag along posing as a signaller mapping out radio dead spots, taking shit off the grunts for not being a 'proper soldier'. The majority of our time there was spent carrying out these mundane tasks, mostly just to blend in with the regulars though some reports occasionally held a certain amount of significance. If we had of spent our days sitting round doing fuck all, not only would people start wondering who exactly we were but, as individuals we would have started slipping up on all sorts of drills. It doesn't matter how experienced or skilled a person is, if he or she stops doing what they do for any extended period of time they will lose their edge. Therefore we got involved wherever we could.

The majority of covert operations in Theatre were carried out by the Special Air Service Regiment, they were the top dogs when it came to this sort of thing. I was assured by my CO that my name was on the list to attend various training courses carried out by these boys but as yet I had not heard anything. The other FO's with me were more than suited to the tasks. Three of them were ex SAS and the other two had completed numerous courses on various aspects of the trade. I was by far the odd one out and it was because of this that I would always find myself wondering how I could have ended up with such an important role having had only the bare minimum of training. I would occasionally pose the question to the others who didn't appear to consider it unusual. Since they had all clearly been in the game a hell of a lot longer than myself I decided not to let it bother me and just take advantage of the additional knowledge I was learning daily.

It took a month or so of male bonding in the various makeshift NAAFI's of Vitez and its nearby outstations to make reasonable friends out of the other five. We would never mix with any members of the occupying regiments purely to avoid any tricky questions, in no way did we compare to the COP Platoons back in Northern Ireland.

If the camp was occupied by Infantry we wore Signals berets, if it was occupied by Signals we wore Engineers berets. Our presence was always made known to the highest ranking officer on site and he would know nothing of any details, just to see we weren't bothered in any way by any of his men. At the time the camp was occupied by 1st Battalion the Cheshire Regiment We would have our own room or porta-cabin and everyone on camp was totally oblivious to the real reason we were there.

Rank meant nothing to any of the six of us, we respected each other in every way we needed to and the fact that we were all good at our job was enough for each of us. For the record though, there was myself, then a Sergeant, Warren a Staff Sergeant thou being ex Infantry he preferred Colour Sergeant, three Captains, Kev Pete and Chris and Ox, who was a Major. He did all the reporting back to the Foreign Office MI6 or whoever it was we were working for. One of us had to take that responsibility and this was probably the only area where rank came into it. Our orders came from him and any details, however trivial, we made him aware of. We were as professional as we could be and operating like the rest of the Army, although a proven method over hundreds of years, wasn't going to make us any more professional. Anyway, although still technically in the Army every day that passed made me feel less like I was. If it wasn't for the fact I walked round camp in combats I'd have felt like I had been de-mobbed months ago.

September brought with it more sunshine and the much anticipated first Op, for me at least. On the second Wednesday, shortly after a leisurely nine o'clock breakfast Ox requested our presence in the tin box to discuss a task handed to us from the Bat Phone. The Army had bought hundreds of steel freight containers which were converted into four man bed sits. The large steel doors removed from the front and replaced with a window and a smaller door. Quite a practical idea I always thought. They provided shelter from any rain or snow in the winter and casseroled us in the summer. From fifteen hundred feet Vitez looked for all the world like a steel housing estate. We had two of these units between us, a stones throw from the main building near the gym. Whenever we needed a briefing we would gather in Ox's which we called the 'tin box'. I can never remember why.

Target 12 as we so affectionately called him was as Captain in the Serbian 'Special Police'. you couldn't count on five sets of hands how many men women and children he had personally executed. To this day I don't know what he did that caused his fate and I don't care. His name doesn't matter either. He was a piece of the puzzle whose time in the game had reached its end. The only thing that still bothered me was why the SAS hadn't been given the job. Ox had known the reason all along and I was on a need to know basis only, today I needed to know.

He didn't actually disclose which department we were working for, only that the SAS weren't involved because we were operating on a slightly different frequency. As it turned out the five of them had worked their way to where they were through years of graft and gaining trust of whoever was on the end of Ox's telephone. I was here purely because of my ability to remember facts and figures faces and names. I was surprised that it didn't bother them in the slightest that I had bypassed these years simply by possessing such an ability, thou on reflection they were far too professional for childish jealousy. Each of them were quite open about how impressed they were that I could remember week old grid references and batch numbers of various aerial imagery, they were glad to have me on board and since I was only just finding out that they knew all about me, yet had been so welcoming over the past few months, made it clear to me that they were nothing but genuine.

CHAPTER 5

Most of the high priority possible targets were already well researched. Researching them after all, was one of the main tasks that filled our days. We focused mainly on targets one to twenty. The closer to one being more important. After twenty we cooled off a bit, to be honest these guys were usually pretty safe. Although jumping right up the table to a top five spot from twenty odd was not that irregular. It all depended on what they had been up to and how the suits back in the UK viewed it.

Our task was pretty simple. Make observations on as many bad guys as possible and pass the Intel to Ox. He would then encrypt it and send it home, probably to some rented office in Canary Wharf. The humanoids there would decode it and pass it onto the suits down the river who would decide how important it was. Then like the Pepsi Network Chart the names on their list would shuffle around and on occasion one would be sent back to us so we could go give them the bad news.

What I had done over here so far had been easy but the time had come to earn the extremely slender paycheque they had been giving me the last few months.

I knew two or three minutes into the O-Group that this guy's demise was about to be planned and executed by the six of us. The only thing I was pretty certain of was that it was unlikely to be me who pulled the trigger. These guys had done this for years, and I was far from ready to be that involved.

I didn't really know what to think or feel. I expected to feel sick but the excitement kept the nausea at bay. The only negative feeling I can remember from that sunny September morning was being slightly anxious at the fact I might lose my own life. I had worried about this to an extent every time I approached the loading bay back in Northern Ireland. On exiting the camp the patrol would double time for the first fifty meters or so as this was a favoured kill zone for any enemy snipers. Between the loading bay and the end of the gauntlet run I would sometimes find myself wondering how I was to end my days. Was it now? Is this my last patrol? At first it was pure fear, then after the first few patrols it turned to a healthy state of awareness.

It wasn't so much fear this time as lack of knowledge. Different questions were presenting themselves that I hadn't needed to ask myself in Ireland. How close was I going to get to the target? Would I stay here or go with the trigger man? This time though I knew how to control it. I was only afraid of the unknown again. Like the first patrol in Ireland, after a few I was fine I just had to keep it together for my first time and possibly the second and third. After that I was sure I would be lapping it up again. The huge responsibility and the thrill of working under covert conditions helped me to keep my cool and settle into the planning.

The Op saw the six of us split into three groups of two. Ox and Chris would remain at Vitez monitoring the whole thing from the 'Tin Can' via comms with Kev and Pete, who would take the responsibility of Insertion and Extraction, leaving Warren and Yours truly as Sniper and Spotter. I should have expected to be part of the Kill Team but even so something in the back of my head kept telling me that to them I was still the Sprog and I'd be staying back at camp to see how they did things. However I was here for my ability to ID targets and all of them had the up most confidence in me. None of them so much as raised an eyebrow when Ox appointed me Spotter.

Most of our Intel on the target was up to date we just had to confirm his habits and daily routines. His role in the Special Police saw him move around the Theatre regularly at random, because of this we couldn't plan to slot him while he was working. Every two to three weeks though he would return home to the village of Gornji Ribnik where what was left of his fellow villagers knew not of his chosen profession. All they would ever see of him was when he returned home, getting out of his car to the laughter and cheers of his five year old son and eight year old daughter who were overjoyed to see their dad after his spell away. Who knew what cover story he had to keep his wife and kids loving him the way they did. I'm sure if they knew how many families he had destroyed they would not feel so affectionate towards him. He would never return home in uniform which always made me wonder if they even knew that he was a police officer.

Near to his home was a very important British Army Rebro Station. One of the less obvious ones that we liked to keep quiet. Rebro is short for Re-broadcasting for those who didn't know. These stations would act as satellites to send our units radio signals around the Theatre. This Rebro Station was the reason this guy had to be taken out.

Gornji Ribnik was only really a stones throw away from Croat controlled territory, it always confused me as to why this guy kept his family so close to the enemy. As it happens I was correct in assuming it would only be a matter of time before harm would creep over the Inter-entity boundary line and get him. A friend of a friend's uncle's sister's boyfriend or something, had passed onto our intelligence agencies that the Croats had found his families whereabouts and were planning to kill all four of them with an artillery attack. This action of course could potentially damage our Rebro Station and therefore the best course of action would be to do the job ourselves and blame the Muslims or a jealous girlfriend. The time scale of the Croat's attack was estimated to be six weeks as they had to displace artillery to do it and at the time they had bigger fish to fry.

Since his weekend leave was timed last minute and we had no inside knowledge of when he chose to take it we had to plan the Op for two weekends. We knew from his pattern that if he didn't come home after two weeks he would after the third. The best way for us to play it was to be in place on the second weekend and if he didn't return, abort until the third. Getting into the village was straight forward the extraction however required a bit more planning.

Gornji Ribnik village is situated at the top of a rather steep hill with really only one road to it. We could literally walk up to it two days before dressed as locals and lie up until H-hour. Everyone was far too pre-occupied to even bat an eyelid at us. Getting out of the place after blowing a hole in someone would prove more difficult.

During our numerous Recce patrols over the previous months I had found that most, if not all the villages I had visited were like ghost towns. Most of the men had gone away to fight in the conflict and any others killed by it. Teenagers who were lucky enough had fled to colleges in Croatia and any young children that hadn't been orphaned were kept indoors for their own safety. One of the few social groups who made themselves visible to us was the elderly. Safety was the least of their concerns at this point of their lives. The highlight of their day would be the walk to the bottom of the hill to fill what plastic bottles they could find with water. If they were really lucky a passing patrol might take them up on their offer of coffee or something stronger.

Many times was I part of a Regular patrol who called into native's house for coffee. We would all squash up onto the couch, which was always as old as Ox, trying our hardest not to get any mud on the tatty piece of carpet that covered the floorboards, floorboards which were coated in a fifty year old layer of grime. The nineteen seventy's tele would be sitting were it had sat for the past twenty years either showing a barely visible news report or not working at all due to no electricity.

The lines in the old ladies face would tell you a story of years of heart ache and suffering and she would sit there content, silently smiling as we drank the last of her coffee. Which was probably the most expensive item in her food cupboard and was given to us without any thought for the cost.

We couldn't understand her and she couldn't understand us. The interpreter would do his bit for a while but in the end all she wanted was something to break up the day. Making nine cups of coffee for some passing soldiers would numb the pain of her loneliness for a good few hours after we left. So we would sit there obliging her, making out that it was the best cup of coffee we'd ever had. Even if it did taste like boiled shit.

Just before the hill's summit was a school, behind this was a clearing then a scattering of houses here and there. Some which were smashed to pieces and others which were occupied. The population of the village was so sparse that we could literally walk into one of the unoccupied houses during the night and not risk being seen. Even if we were seen, we would probably just be mistaken for locals looking for resources in the broken down houses.

At six o'clock on a summery Thursday night we were dropped at the foot of the hill by Kev and Pete in an old smacked up open back pick up truck. I had brown flared corduroy pants a knitted woolly jumper, like the one your Nan gets your Dad for Christmas and a green rain Mac. I have to add that I was considerably better dressed than Warren. My footwear was black steel toe capped safety shoes one with the original lace and one tied with bail twine. I was more scared of the uphill walk ahead of us than I was of being rumbled.

For the firearm fans among you Warren's weapon of choice for this Op was the M-93 Black Arrow. Not that he had much choice. Ox decided on it because it was Yugoslavian built meaning that there was plenty of them in the country, it wasn't in any way linked to us and it was nice and heavy for us to carry up the hill. It had a particular heavy barrel to assist in the accurate path of the fired projectile. Being .50 calibre it had a considerably large energetic potential. In English, it could take your fuckin' head off. It had an effective killing range of 1600m, since we were aiming to be about 750 to 800 away from the target it would still be going nice and fast when it hit him.

We each had a pile of firewood. Various meter and a half lengths of different shapes. The Arrow was stored in its wooden case in the middle of the wood. The case itself looked for the entire world like another piece of wood. We had our side arms in the event that we were compromised and I had my Binos in my woodpile. We had no radio or form of communication. We knew the routes by foot to three extraction points. Should we fail to make it to the first at the said time we would divert to the second and so on. If we missed the third we were on our own until Ox could sort it, we couldn't risk being caught with any link to the Mob. Warren spoke fluent Serbo-Croat and I just had to play the dumb mute to any natives we came across. On completion the weapon and binos were to be left behind for the scene of crime investigators to hopefully come to an incorrect conclusion and hey presto the Op would be complete and any lose ends tied up. That was the theory any how.

The tab up the hill seemed to take a life time and although the majority of areas on my feet had over the years become immune to blisters, the new footwear I was sporting managed to put some in places I hadn't had any before. The speed and distance was nothing out of the ordinary, I'd walked ten times the distance at ten times the pace more times than I could ever count. Some how though I found myself more out of breath than I'd ever been. My heart was beating faster than it had ever on any other forced march or run and the sweat was dripping off me. At the time I remember thinking what a pain in the arse time to come down with a flu bug but on reflection the only thing wrong with me was an adrenaline overdose. Northern Ireland was Northern Ireland and over the years I'd started to look at it as an ordinary job. Not that it had become boring but I'd done that many tours that I knew the drills inside out. This was totally different it was all new to me and I was in as deep as I could get. I knew I had to calm down though, not only for the sake of the job but also if Warren spotted it he'd probably start thinking he'd been paired with an over excited school kid.

By the time we reached our lay up point I was fine. The site we had chosen was an old stone cottage on the east side of the hill. Set around eighty to a hundred meters to the nearest occupied house it was as derelict as it could be. What little rendering was left on the external walls was riddled with bullet holes and in the main living space inside weeds grew through the rubble were the floorboards once lay. Locals had fleeced the place of anything they could burn to keep warm during the bitterly cold winters. The outhouse or coal shed looked out over a clearing of two hundred meters the other side of which was a small hamlet of houses. Behind these was a larger clearing of six hundred meters, all of which was down hill and home to the odd copse. We had to fire in between the houses and along side one of the larger copses. Although we had a clear line of sight to the target the area, before and after the houses and trees could prove to contain enough drafts to send our message off course, so the shot wasn't going to be as clear cut as we'd hoped. However over the last few days the weather had been gorgeous and there wasn't a hint of the slightest breeze so we were confidant.

We spent that night organising our foxhole. We removed three bricks for Warren and one for Myself. Warren chose to adopt the prone position for the shot so his opening was low down in the wall and was hidden by the grass and weeds that had grown up the outside wall. My opening was barely visible and since we were both set back from the wall there was unlikely to be any noticeable reflection from the sight glass. What we had to be careful of was any grass obstructing the barrel. As unbelievable as it may sound a blade of grass would be enough to send the projectile off course by a meter or so over an eight hundred meter range.

I didn't like to ask Warren what would become of any locals that stumbled across us now. In the O Group we were simply told to avoid them. If they did mention a solution to contact I missed it. I just hoped non would come. I wasn't as cold hearted back then as I would become.

We stayed up most of the night whispering old Army stories to each other, though Warren did most of the talking as his tales were quite a bit more interesting than mine. Stories of Beirut and Iran during the Eighties humbled my petrol bomb riots in West Belfast and since I knew this I gave the respectful 'Wow' every now and then.

As we expected no locals even came into sight. So much so, that as an observer of the Op you would think we had the wrong village. As the 4 am witching hour approached the tiredness kicked in. Not enough to affect the drills, but we didn't know what was going to happen after the shot was fired. We could end up tabbing and evading enemy forces for days, so the best plan was to get as much sleep in now as we could. The target wasn't expected until the next night or even the morning after that, if indeed he was coming this week at all. We did an hour on hour off through to lunch time the following day, taking the stag in turns. Around one in the afternoon we had cheese and biscuits which Warren had stashed in his pockets. We had taken them out of their wrappers so we wouldn't have to leave any trace or be found with them on us since they were Army issue ration pack biscuits. The cheese was slices of Red Leicester out the cookhouse which also wasn't in any wrapping. The coat Warren had on was a donkey jacket out of an aid parcel. Despite the scorching weather the locals will still wear woolly jumpers and big coats so we had no choice. The cheese had been in the pocket of the donkey jacket uncovered for the best part of twenty hours. It was sweaty and covered in fluff and dust and still went down a treat with a few mouthfuls of lukewarm water.

The afternoon was again spent sharing stories and basic banter and like the previous night there wasn't a sign of any unwanted guests, apart from a crooked old lady about four hundred meters away who came out around two o'clock to hang some sheets out in the mid day sun.

Less than half an hour later she came out again to take them in, which could give you some indication of how hot the place was. There was also occasional movement around the hamlet and further on towards the target's house but nothing in the immediate area. It looked like we were going to go unnoticed through out the entire Op. The exit route also, which tracked further up the hill and over the top in the direction of Croatia tended to be quiet and short of locals. All these pointers led to us feeling a lot more comfortable about the whole thing. The key to a smooth care free Op is good planning and accurate Intel. Since both were as they should be our job was going to be a great deal easier. I just hoped Warren was as good a shot as the others had told me he was. The last thing we needed was to be pumping off two or three shots or even having to reload as the target ducked and dived behind anything he could find and his wife and kids came running out screaming and crying as we put holes were ever we could, desperately trying to turn him off.

We had zeroed the weapon on the way up with Kev and Pete, on a desolate stretch of road between Jajce and Mrkonjic-Grad and within seven shots he had his grouping down to half an inch over four hundred meters. This was all well and good but since we only wanted one shot to be fired grouping wasn't an issue. He had to get it right first time.

We reckoned that from the target's vehicle first coming in to our scope and him parking up and getting out we had about two to two and a half minutes which was plenty of time to make any elevation and wind allowances on the sight.

A little after nine o'clock the blue and white Suzuki Vitara came into sight. I blew Dixie and Warren was ready to go in seconds. Before I could say anything about the wind or elevation Warren gave me the nod he was all set. I tracked the vehicle back to the house keeping an eye out for any bystanders who could mess the job up in any way as Warren would have to remain focused on the vehicle. We lost him briefly as he passed behind the Hamlet then came to a stop in the opening, exactly were we predicted. He exited the car and hung around for a moment at the side, taking out his bag. With the car between us and him all we could see was the top of his head. We weren't going to risk a head shot, most snipers very rarely do. That's just shit you see in the movies. You put your shot in the centre of the mass because you have less chance of missing. Plus I hadn't identified him yet.

He moved to the front and placed his bag on the bonnet. Facing us I was able to I.D. him straight away. He looked just like his photo, hadn't changed a bit.

"It's him, when you're ready." I said.

Warren wanted to wait to see if he moved away from the vehicle a bit more. As it stood, if we didn't kill him with one he could fall behind the car and we would be unable to hit him with a second.

When the weapon discharged I was thinking that his kids must have been in bed as they were not there to greet him. I was still thinking it when he fell half way up his garden path. The shot was flawless, it hit him in his lower back and at a guess I would say you could fit a large turnip in the exit wound. Even if he didn't die straight away there was no way anyone was going to save him. I watched him through the binos for a while to check his status and observed zero movement. Job done.

We picked up the piles of firewood and set off further up the hill. About half a click up we came to a sawmill where we broke track and dumped the wood. We tabbed for just over and hour through the rough on a north westerly heading and arrived at the rendezvous where Kev and Pete were waiting in the pick up. We got ourselves comfy in the back as the truck set off after a brief greeting and confirmation of the kill to the others. I hadn't given the death a second thought until this point.

CHAPTER 6

The moon seemed huge that night and there were more stars in the sky than I had ever seen. The journey back to Vitez took almost three hours as we had to keep our speed down to avoid attracting attention and stay off the main drags to avoid anyone on their way to the crime scene.

During the long trip back, sat in the back of the pick up, along with hoping we didn't get stopped I found myself wondering if I was feeling guilty. I couldn't decide if it was guilt or shock. I just couldn't stop going over the whole thing. I had seen plenty of people who had just died and plenty of month-old bodies. I'd even been just around the corner when an off duty RUC officer had a heart attack and attempted to revive him for forty minutes until the ambulance came only to be told later that he was dead before he hit the ground. I'd been around death plenty but I'd never actually stared him in the eyes.

As I looked through the binos down the hill at the target all I can remember seeing was his coat twitch and his body arch briefly backwards before it fell forward. For those three hours though I went over it so many times, I couldn't understand why. I kept telling myself to forget it. Ok so it was my first involvement in a killing but get over it, you have just done Bosnia a huge favour. When I couldn't stop thinking about how his kids were going to be, opening the door to find their dad's eight pints running down the garden path I starting wondering if I was in the right job.

So he was a bad person, they didn't know that. To them he was their hero. As bad as he was, he probably gave his kids all the love in the world when he came home to them. The way they would run down the path towards him told me that. Now their hero was gone and I was pretty sure they wouldn't understand why for many years to come. I played a part in doing that to those kids regardless of what other kids I had saved from the same fate.

Stop. The other kids. I'd forgot about them. What about all the other families that would have suffered if he had been allowed to live? What about the families he had destroyed and gone unpunished for? It slowly began to make sense. It was a numbers game. What is better, a hundred families suffering or just one? Just one of course. I was a necessary evil, I had just forgotten briefly. My job was one of the most important in the world I told myself. If there was a God I was an ambassador for him on Earth. Like Priests and Ministers, they are the office staff who promote the theory and I was a labourer who did the necessary dirty work. That however sounds like the thoughts of a psychopath and anyway I don't believe in God.

Ok. If there isn't a God what about the battle between good and evil? I was definitely holding some serious rank on the good side wasn't I? Fair enough the good people, however you put it to them will tell you that killing is wrong but I'd just stopped a lot of it by doing it myself. Would they see that though? I doubt it.

Alright, so I wasn't good. I wasn't bad either because I still think I did it to stop further suffering.

I cant keep up. Where the hell was I? I looked around for a moment. Warren was staring too. I hoped so much that he was where I was. I didn't ask him though. I didn't like to share thoughts like that with anyone.

I returned to the chicken soup, which is what I felt my head was full of. I had to make some sense of what I was doing before I did it again or I might go mad.

Ok. From the top. Who did I work for? British Intelligence. Though it was no good trying to find comfort in saying they knew what they were doing. We just blew a hole in someone on their command to save some radios from getting blown up. So who do I work for? God? Load of bollocks, if he exists he is as sick and twisted as the rest of us. Come on think. Who am I doing this for? The only thing certain in life is death and taxes. Ok. Well I'm pretty certain the Inland Revenue couldn't give a shit if Target Twelve lived or died so that left Death.

That night, sitting there undisturbed in my thoughts for all that time I came to the conclusion that my new found skill had been in me all along. I have never liked the thought that we are not in control of our own destiny but I came to believe that everyone has a date and time assigned to them and nothing you can do will change this. Be it a car accident or one of my bullets, when your number gets called your time is up like it or not.

I built a make believe company in my head that was responsible for processing people from this world and transporting them to the next. Mr Reaper was Company Director and I was on the shop floor. Good or bad everyone got processed sooner or later and when it was their turn either myself the sick and twisted serial killer the car accident or whatever means was assigned to the task. Fair enough the order at the moment came from the Government but ultimately it was Death Inc. who signed for it.

This worked for me for now, I was still only twenty six and hadn't been in the Army nine years yet so I should really be honoured to find myself in such a responsible role at such a young age. Formalities like Death Inc. should really be brushed under the carpet and I should be concentrating on showing some gratitude for where my life had taken me. I may just have been a piece in a big game of chess but it wasn't just Brigade Commanders playing now it was entire Countries and the prizes were not just press articles they were human lives. I was considered by someone, professional enough to be assigned to the task of eliminating key figures in a war of nations. So I did what I thought best at the time. I snapped out of my episode of self concern and applied myself to the job at hand. From that day on things started running like a Swiss clock.

CHAPTER 7

In July 93 almost a year to the day that I was deployed to Bosnia I found out I was leaving. Ox told me over a gristly beef stroganoff in the cookhouse on what I think was a Friday. After three weeks leave I was to report to Bulford camp again to be briefed on my new posting or assignment as I was beginning to call it. As far as I knew it was only myself and Kev who were being re-assigned. I didn't ask about the others, I wasn't really arsed. I knew I had made some friends here and wherever we were in the world, if we ever bumped into each other again I'd have someone to go the pub with.

Kev had to report to Catterick so I knew wherever I was going I would be meeting new people again. Ox didn't have to tell me that all though we are all in the same game, you never talk to new faces about the old ones. You keep the memories for yourself.

Where the leave was concerned I knew where I was going to spend it, for two reasons mainly. Usually when leave came a gang of us would jump a plane to Benidorm or some other sunny concrete jungle but I hadn't seen those guys for two years. I wasn't going to ask Kev to come on a sunny holiday with me. For one, we didn't have that sort of relationship. It was purely professional. Secondly if I had of asked he would have just called me a fag and chinned me.

The other reason was the prominent one. I hadn't spent any lengthy amount of time at home since I signed up. When I say home I mean the city itself. There wasn't really a house there I could call home anymore.

Liverpool. No matter what I did or who I killed I knew I would always feel welcome there. I almost felt as though I owed it to the place to go visit. Something about the closely built streets and the tight knit communities seems to offer some form of shelter to the 'ordinary decent criminal' or the individual with a secret to hide. Don't get me wrong, if you commit a crime against the people Scousers are the first to make you sorry for it. Mess with kids or try and rape or mug an old lady and its over for you but steal a lorry load of Kappa trackies or mobile phones and you could flog them all from a Liverpool pub safe in the knowledge you wouldn't have the busies feelin' ya collar. Things are changing nowadays mind, kids in the city today aren't respectful of their elders and the age old rules of the streets of Liverpool are sadly becoming folklore. The old school villains who crack the little shits round the back of the head for being gobby are a dying breed.

All my school friends would have grown up and forgotten me and my parents had emigrated, all that was left was my Mum's Brother Jeff. I didn't have a clue what he was doing now but I knew he would let me stay if I needed to. I hadn't seen much of him in the last nine years but when I had he would take me down to his local and get me to tell him stories of Northern Ireland then brag to his mates how his nephew was a big brave soldier. I liked him, I knew there was no harm in him and he would be more than happy for me to stay. That's providing he was still living in the same house if indeed he hadn't been processed yet.

The plan was to turn up at his house and ask him out for a drink. When we got out and he asked where I was staying I'd say "hotel" and he'd reply "Fuck off, Y' can doss at ours". Great stuff.

I hadn't spent any money for a year so my account was chocker. With this in mind I got a 'Blackie' from Manchester airport after coming from Split to Brize Norton and then from Luton to Manchester. Having been awake for thirty six hours the cab wasn't even on the motorway and I was falling asleep. I awoke startled with the 'Cabbie' asking me 'where abouts' I wanted. I gave him the address and started to come round. The first thing I saw that made me feel at home was The Rocket at the end of the M62. We turned right onto Queens Drive and headed towards Walton. The place hadn't changed at all, apart from the odd new building and renovation. I loved it here. I sat up in the back of the cab like a tourist on his first visit. There was a much quicker way to get to where we were going but I didn't care. I was loaded and I loved seein' all the old sights again.

We passed Walton Hospital on the left and The Plough, Jeff's local on the opposite side. After the old Dunlop's Building we turned right onto Stalmine Road. Jeff lived about half way down on the right.

I was greeted at the door by my Aunty Pauline who was overjoyed at the sight of me. From the first second she was fussing over me. Taking my bags and sitting me down. I hadn't been in the house a full three minutes and she was making me some butty's and a cup of tea. The whole thing felt strange but I relished it all the same. I knew I belonged in the game for now, yet some how the spam butty's Kwik Save's own plain crisps and the tinted glass mug of tea reassured me that, after all said and done I was a working class Scouser and Liverpool would always welcome me home.

After what I considered to be a reasonable amount of time giving my attention to Pauline I asked where Jeff was.

With all the logistics of the last two days I had completely forgotten that the football season had just started again and it was half three on a Saturday afternoon. It was a home game so there was only one place Jeff was going to be and that was Goodison Park.

After the match he and his mates would catch the bus back down to the Plough for a couple of hour's worth of alcohol. Depending on whether the Blues won or lost would determine whether they would go out again after tea. Pauline was great. For most home games she would make a big pan of Scouse for the lot of them accompanied by a full loaf of buttered Warburton's toastie and if that wasn't enough do the washing up before she followed Jeff down to the pub later on. He was always smashed by the time she got there so she would just drink twice as much twice as fast to catch up.

Jeff would work all the hours he could in the week at the Jacob's factory to keep them living a basic but comfortable life. The balance between the two of them where contributions to the running of the house were concerned was perfect. Their two daughters were about my age and had flown the nest some years ago, though visited regularly. During the week Pauline would shop and do house work and Jeff would work his shifts and come home with his tea ready and everything that needed doing, done. The soaps would fill their week day nights until

Friday when it was a 'chippy tea' and some cans together. You couldn't find a more typical, content working class family if you looked all your life.

When I asked if I could leave my bags in the hall while I went for a pint with Jeff, unbeknown to Pauline I had started phase one of the accommodation plot. "How long are you home for?" she asked. "A few weeks, I'm gonna get a hotel in town and just chill out for a while."

I knew damn well she wouldn't hear of that. She suggested I stay there and save my money to go to a game or two and get them both pissed a few times. That was fine by me, though it would have probably been cheaper to stay at the Adelphi than promise to get them two pissed a few times. Money was never an issue with me though. I could take it or leave it. As long as I could afford food and shelter the rest was anybody's.

I walked down to the Plough and sat there at the bar with a pint of lager and waited for Jeff and his mates to return. I recognised some of the faces from my previous visits, though not enough to let on to them. I could see some of them looking and probably thinking the same. I knew as soon as Jeff came in they would be over saying; "I thought it was you." Meanwhile they were happy just to sit in the same stool they had for years and sip bitter or mild out of a glass they had probably drank from a thousand times.

I could see within half an hour why I hadn't just taken a job at Jacob's and married some fit bird. Although it was a novelty for me to be home I was happy just visiting. Maybe one day I would find the need to spend my days sitting on a bar stool all day, staring down the eighteen year old barmaid's top. I would never slag that life style off. It just wasn't for me. Not yet anyway.

When Jeff came in it was party time. Whatever happened at the football didn't matter anymore. It was Saturday night and his favourite nephew was home. He gave one of the local scallys 50p to run home and tell Pauline to "fuck tea off and come out for a drink." Before long we were full of lager and tequila and laughing and joking like I'd never been away. Sure enough the curious bar flies were over with the predicted line and I was soon being pressed for some Army stories, which from now on I had to make up.

In the weeks that followed I would take walks into Walton Park to walk around the duck pond or the bus into town for some new jeans. I suppose some would say I needed the rest and maybe I could have used the time to reflect on whether or not it was right to turn off that guy in Ribnik village. These few weeks were really the last chance I had to change the course of my life before the doors closed behind me. I hadn't yet processed anyone myself, just assisted. I'm sure if I had wanted to I could still have gotten out of the game. This wasn't the CIA I was working for I was just in the Army. I wasn't going to take one in the back of the head as I went for my Sunday paper because of the things I had witnessed.

However back then I wasn't anywhere near to that frame of mind. After the first week all I could think about was getting back and where I would be going. It could have been anywhere and the excitement of this was making me wish my leave wasn't so long.

I ran every morning, along the old loop line towards Hartley's, up and over onto Long lane and round the main roads back to Stalmine. All the places I would go as a kid.

Pauline rang my parents in New Zealand on one of the nights and handed the phone over. I had spoke to them on occasion on the phone or sometimes with a letter. Each time we spoke though they felt more like strangers. Now when we spoke it was more like speaking to old friends than it was my Mum and Dad.

When it was time to leave the city again I got the old 'Don't leave it so long next time' speech. I told them how grateful I was for letting me stay, did the whole kiss on the cheek and hand shake thing and walked off up the street like Auntie's brave soldier.

I caught a bus into town and walked up from Paradise Street to the train station. It was nearly ten years since I had caught a train from Liverpool Lime Street and for the second time in ten years it would be taking me to the same destination. The Unknown.

CHAPTER 8

As I flashed my ID card to the guard at Bulford camp it was as though a huge weight had been lifted off my shoulders. I was so glad to be back. I reported straight to my Commanding Officer who sent me directly to the Quarter Master to sign for some accommodation. I was allocated a room in the Sergeants Mess and spent the night getting my shit together.

I had all ready been debriefed on Bosnia but the next morning I had an informal talk about as much as I could with the Colonel. If any awkward questions were asked I would simply tell him they *were* and he was fine with that. He knew that regardless of his rank over me he had no authority to insist on answers to awkward questions. He asked how I was finding the whole transfer thing now I had been with them for a couple of years and I obliged him with honest answers. The whole morning was very informal, he even sent a runner out for bacon on toast for the two of us to have eleven's together. We sat there in his office which overlooked a drill square as he went through Ox's evaluation of me. He seemed more than impressed and went on to tell me that my next posting would involve a much more comfortable working environment. No dusty roads or blistering heat and no late night recce's in the freezing snow. All items of green clothing would be left here and instead I was to be issued a shit load of NEXT vouchers. Intrigued? Not really. I was more worried that I'd be sitting in an airport or something for the next six months.

I had two months before I was to be deployed and these were spent getting me on as many training courses as possible. Although my experience was beginning to grow I was still in need of various courses simply because that's the way things are done. The courses were boring as usual but educational just the same. The Small Arms Handling course showed me how to operate more side arms than I care to mention. From Glocks to Rugers by the end of the course I felt I could pick up anything a find my way around it in less than a couple of seconds. My marks on the Observation Management course were amusing, to me at least. One of the tests would involve being put in a pitch black room which was set out like a grocers shop. The lights would come on for sixty seconds and you were allowed to look around. After the lights went out you would be removed from the room and asked to do a variety of physical tasks like running or beep tests. Then you would be put in a quiet room with a piece of paper. On it would be questions like how many tins of spaghetti were in the basket at the checkout or what the headline on the newspapers was. Until I came the highest score was 63%. I never scored less than 85%. The instructors were convinced I had a method and ask me to tell them about it, but I honestly didn't.

I packed all my military kit into MFO boxes which were put into storage for me. When I had days off I would get the duty driver to run me into Salisbury to spend my NEXT vouchers. Shirts and ties, smart trousers and shoes. No jeans. These were far from my kind of clothes; I was more a jeans t-shirt and trainers person. This was business though and after a Nancy boy hair cut and a shave I pulled it off ok. I bought one of those fold over suit bags and a briefcase for hand luggage and wouldn't you know it the CO told me to try and tone down my accent. He described it as talking with a mouthful of milkshake and jokingly informed me that nothing 'posh' ever came out of Liverpool. I went on to tell him that when rich people travelled by ship from Liverpool they would be issued a ticket with the abbreviation POSH on it. This stood for Port Out Starboard Home. Which meant that they would have a cabin on the port side on the outward journey and starboard on the way home, meaning that the sun would always shine through their window. Therefore the very word 'Posh' comes from Liverpool. He called me a bullshitting bastard to which I replied; "I believe the word is Gobshite La'." He told me I would never get promoted if I continued to talk like that to my superior officers.

I left from Heathrow Airport business class to Dulles International Airport in Washington around 9am on a Tuesday morning. I had never even seen a business class compartment let alone travelled in one. It was quite ridiculous how much I was pampered during the flight. After becoming accustomed to the back of a four toner or sleeping rough in coal sheds, the a la carte menu, fizzy wine and spacious leather seats felt, well strange. I must admit I did enjoy the whole experience and I told myself; as long as I don't let it make me soft, then why the fuck not.

I had been assigned to the British Embassy in Washington. At least that was my address while I was in town. I would be working in close conjunction with a member of America's National Security Staff. I know it all sounds very boring and the words 'desks' and 'nine to five' come to mind again but this time there was a bit of a deal involved.

The Colonel had informed me that this posting was to be around eighteen months long with possible extensions. The task was sharing Intel with the Americans in order to increase the UN's databases on various members of the warring factions in the former Yugoslavia. Yeah I know, boring. The deal however had a side which was beneficial to me. I would spend my days travelling from my hotel on New York Avenue to my place of work just around the corner on Massachusetts Avenue. Most days it was just eight to five though some days involved business dinners, depending on the classification of the information we were discussing. All very civilised stuff and to be honest far to posh for me.

In return for all this mundane routine I was to be put on as many different training courses as possible, whenever they could fit me in. Although I always considered British training to be the best something about the offer appealed to me. It was only eighteen months of my life and attending courses ran by the FBI and the CIA could do nothing but benefit me in the future. There would be time for more field work, right now I knew that I was doing pretty well on experience but lacked the formal training. This was the ideal opportunity to improve my career prospects.

I had the respect of the training teams from day one. The Americans love the British and although they struggled to warm to my sarcastic sense of humour at first, it soon grew on them.

The job itself, although very tedious did have its perks. Any time we had to, we would jump a business class flight to New York to visit United Nations Plaza for any meetings or briefs they felt we need to attend. My Oppo Anthony knew all the places to go in both Washington and New York. He was about fifty or so and very cultured. I doubt very much whether he had seen any action but never the less he knew his job inside out and his knowledge of British and American military history at some points totally overwhelmed me.

The next couple of years really were a turning point for me. As hard as I tried not to I found myself enjoying drinking the brandy in 'Jean Georges' French restaurant in Trump Tower and walking round East Manhattan in the suits I had put on the expenses account. At the same time though it was always in the back of my head that I could become too attached to the whole thing and lose my edge.

I stayed on top of my fitness at all times and whenever I was on a course, I would remember who I was and how to stay that person. By the middle of my third year in Washington I could speak fluent Spanish and excellent Serbo-Croat. I had just achieved my purple belt in Brazilian Jiu Jitsu, in which I attended classes three nights a week and most of Saturday at the FBI Training Academy at Quantico, which was about an hour outside of Washington. Work were extremely understanding when it came to my courses, all I had to do was mention to Anthony I was at a class and it was fine for me to leave early or arrive late. I was learning so much at an alarming rate. It was extremely demanding of both my time and energy but I loved it. I could list the qualifications I acquired whilst at this posting but it would only bore you, if I'm not already. The point here is, Washington was the training I had needed to progress. Whatever Ox and the guys had, I now had. I wasn't the Sprog any more, by anyone's standards.

On the 23rd of May 1996 I attended another one of many cocktail evenings. Like all of these evenings, within half an hour I would find myself gagging for a pint and some working class company to talk footy with. I would stand there in my penguin suit talking shop with various high ranking officials from all departments, trying desperately to show an interest. The highlight of their night would be my accent and the highlight of mine the last sentence of the closing address.

This night however was to be entirely different.

The voice came from behind and said something to the effect of; "Years can change a lot of things about a person, its just a damn shame they cant do anything for the fucking awful accent of yours.

He was right, the years had changed a lot about him too, adding a good few inches to his waste line.

"I see your still makin' full use of the expense account then. Ya fat cunt!" I replied.

It was a good five years since our long talks in the Gatwick Holiday Inn but it felt like only yesterday.

"How ya doin Mike mate?" I asked him.

"Better than you!" he said.

CHAPTER 9

The closing speech came around ten thirty, given by the Director of Bullshit for the United Nations. I know I come across as very unprofessional were this posting is concerned but to be honest I could do my day to day job with my eyes closed. All we had to do was use various methods to extract the Intel from the Theatre and compile it for the United Nations staff. Washington was never about the job it was always about the training. Nights like this were not partaken out of choice believe me.

As we left the building Mike came over and by asking if I wanted to go for a beer, reassured me that the Western World wasn't only being protected by cocktail drinking polo players.

We spent the entire night at an Irish bar catching up on things, talking as much as we could about what we had been up to. The beer flowed as did the laughs and before long the Irish bar was just like the Holiday Inn at Gatwick. As we chatted I again came to realise that Mike was the only real friend I had, though I would never tell him. He wasn't the type to appreciate soppy shite. Sure I had made friends in Ox and the others but they would go their own way after the beer had taken effect, probably without even saying bye. Mike however was the type to see you off in a cab then ring in the morning to talk about how good the night was. Although I never did, I knew if I needed to talk about Ribnik and how it changed my view of stopping life all I had to do was say.

As well as joking and flirting with the bar girls we talked about the job and were it was taking us both. Mike had been pen pushing for the CIA for the past five years, before that he was a Customs Agent for four years and a US Ranger for eleven. He was a good friend to have, especially in this game. He was on the Field Ops planning team at Langley and was the type of character who probably walked around his office with everyone liking him and willing to do favours for him that would usually require a letter from God.

When I say pen pushing I mean he did everything from his office. Just because he didn't put his combats on anymore it didn't mean he couldn't blow up a cocaine factory in Colombia or have a bullet put in some one in Bangkok.

The conversation moved onto whether I saw myself in the British Army until pension day or if I would change departments at any point. I informed him that if he was trying to poach me there was no way the American Government would employ someone like me. The fact that I would be Ex British Intelligence would be enough for them to turn their nose up at me.

"You might be British but don't flatter yourself, your far from intelligent." He said.

"What if you weren't working for the American Government? What if you worked for me?"

As it happened the CIA had a budget solely for spending on outside contractors. Mike would recruit me as an 'Asset' and I would be paid from this budget which took the form of a consultancy company for overhead power cable maintenance. At this point my eyebrows raised a good inch and I gave a decisive "Hmmmmmm!"

I knew the main obstacle; if I decided to take the job, would be working out my years notice for the mob. The Colonel wouldn't be happy about losing me and might pull me back to work out my twelve months back home. When I told Mike of my concerns he just smiled and blew from his nose. He could have letters come from whoever he wanted saying whatever he wanted. All he had to do was have someone in the UN tell my boss how important it was to finish up here and get the best out of me before I left. He could insist on replacing me but I had a feeling he would probably just go along with it. He liked to stay in peoples good books after all.

That was the obstacle sorted, now I just had to decide if it was actually what I wanted. I would be giving up a lot. I had after all worked my bollocks off over the years to get to where I was and who knew how much further I would get when I returned home with all these extra strings to my bow. One thing was for sure I wasn't going to decide after ten pints. Mike had had ten pints too and for all I knew he could have become a very good bullshitter in the last five years. I told him of how I would think about it as I had a lot of things to consider. He just smiled and told me how he would be seeing more of me now anyway.

"Forget about it for now." He said. "We gonna get something to eat or what?"

He loved his food.

The following day was a Friday if I remember correctly. To be honest I only remember this because the cocktail evening started off a very long weekend of partying. The next day at work most of the embassy staff were pissed until after dinner. When two o'clock came a skeleton staff was appointed for the weekend and everyone else carried on with the party. This was of course kept as low key as possible to members of the public.

I spent all day Saturday at Quantico training. I was certain I would be able to achieve my black belt before I was reappointed though this was not to be. For anyone who doesn't know about Brazilian Jiu Jitsu the hardest transition is from blue to purple belt. Since I had recently achieved this I convinced myself I would soon be a black belt, as I would do some form of training every day.

Mike came to Quantico with me to see some old friends. I knew he would have been a popular guy but even so I was surprised at just how many people knew him. He had attended just about every training course on offer and advised on many of them himself.

On Saturday evening Mike invited me back to his place for tea, or dinner as I was supposed to call it now. I met his wife Hailey and his six year old daughter Lauren who were both beautiful people too. His home was tastefully decorated and in the kitchen pots and pans were bubbling away as Hailey rushed around in an apron doing her best to make me feel welcome as she put things in and out of the oven. Mike took me through to his lounge and sat me down. Lauren came over in her little pink pyjamas and asked if I wanted a beer out the fridge. This is my earliest memory of her.

The night sticks in my mind for many reasons. Maybe because it was the night I first met his family or because I had only ever felt this sort of welcome in Liverpool. Or maybe its because, sat there in his red leather sofa when Lauren toddled off for my beer and Mike went to check if Hailey needed any help, I had another one of those moments. The moment itself probably only lasted for a minute to ninety seconds, just the time it took Lauren to get back from the fridge, but it was one of those thoughts that would grow in my mind over the course of the next few hours.

Lauren was the sweetest and most innocent girl you could ever hope to meet. His wife Hailey worked so hard to make the evening enjoyable and still found the energy to insist myself and Mike retired to their huge conservatory while her and Lauren cleaned up. With, I might add, no argument from Lauren. His family was perfect and I couldn't help wondering how he did it. How did he sleep? Did he not worry about whether or not his family would remain safe? Had he ever taken a life and if so how did he stay the loving husband and father he was?

I did like what he had but I was in no way jealous. I assumed one day I would have it all too but for now I was to remain unattached. The thought of that kind of commitment soon put out any paternity fires that might have been starting.

Sat there sipping brandy on his cane furniture, I toyed with the idea of taking the questions to the next level. Should I ask him about his past? Has he done any jobs for Death Inc.? Does he not worry it might endanger Lauren or Hailey? As I drifted back to moment I found Mike staring at me silently.

"Where do you want to go"? He asked.

"We cant go out now" I said "We'll have to at least have a few drinks with Hailey."

"I don't mean that you fukin dope." He replied. "Where do you want your life to take you? What do you want to do with it?"

"Not die any time soon." I said jokingly.

"Why not? What are you scared of?"

I remember saying something about how the conversation was in danger of drifting into one of those deep ones that lasts all night and ends up back where you started. Never the less we continued and found ourselves lost in a world of unproven theories about were we end up and if we do find ourselves being judged by either a God or an Alien. Who built the Pyramids was in there somewhere, along with the devil and reincarnation. We had covered almost everything when he asked me.

"Have you ever killed anyone"? He just came out with it like that.

"You must have done, all them years in Northern Ireland."

"I haven't no" I replied. "Have You?"

"A few yeah." He said.

"How many's a few?" I didn't no whether I was going too far. It certainly felt like I was.

"Enough. I'm happy behind my desk now." I believed him.

The conversation progressed even further than this. About how Hailey knew he worked for the CIA but also knew never to ask any awkward questions. About how I might not have pulled any triggers but definitely had it in me and about how he would walk away before danger got within two continents of his family. We sat there for four hours talking that night, disturbed only once while Hailey wished us goodnight. I can't remember whether I was pissed or not when Mike saw me into my taxi about three in the morning. Whether I was or I wasn't made no difference. The conversations we just had made it clear in my mind that I could follow this path if I wanted to. I had all the skills I needed to be good at it and talking like we did took away any doubts of whether it was right or wrong.

The conclusions we had come to where simple; Smallpox once wiped out millions and we found a solution to it. As soon as we did something else came along. If doctors cure cancer there will be something else. I don't know what the statistics are for the amount of babies born in a minute world wide but I reckon the figure is higher than the amount of deaths. There is only so much space on this planet and Mother Nature knows this. She will always find away of maintaining balance. Death is a part of life. It will happen to everyone. Sometimes if it happens to an individual sooner rather than later it benefits others. Some people are bad to others and some people aren't. Some deserve to live others don't. If Mike wants to give me a hundred thousand dollars to end a life then 'What the fuck?' they're gonna die anyway. I might as well get rich out of it.

CHAPTER 10

It is a very common misconception that the CIA is near impossible to become a part of. Hollywood has given us the picture of it being a highly secret organisation with a place in its ranks being virtually unattainable. I have no doubt that the selection process and training is extremely demanding and the success rate is probably very low. The company can afford to be fussy about who they employ and who they don't, given that the amount of post-graduates who fancy themselves as a secret agent in the States is probably quite high. Their outlook on permanent staff and their contractors however varies widely. When a contractor is recruited the company is thinking words like inexpensive low maintenance and expendable. You might think that at $80,000 to $120,000 a job it is far from cost effective to use a contractor but when you consider the training, twenty years wages, pension contributions expense accounts and medical plans of the permanent staff its Asda price again isn't it.

The company has various levels of contractor available to them. Being that I had never given anyone the bad news I would be at the lowest level. The guy who had been sleeping rough in the Columbian jungle for the last three years with five million dollars in his bank account was at the top level. Despite our varying experience we were both expendable, perhaps not equally but certainly more so than the permanent guy. If the company didn't want to use us any more they could just put one in my head or leave the guy in Columbia to rot, the permanent staff on the other hand tended to just be given a gold clock and a letter of thanks from the chief.

The next few months are still to this day, a blare in my mind. I was so busy that my personal journals were neglected and although I have a good memory I'm only human. I know I saw Mike almost every day and he managed to get me on the register for all sorts of lectures and training courses. The Colonel phoned occasionally to try and get out of me the real reason I wanted to leave. He probably convinced himself, with good reason, that I had been poached by someone. He himself knew what Washington was like. I'm pretty sure that if you sat on a bench near the Reflecting pool between the Lincoln Memorial and the World War Two Memorial for a half hour or so, if fifty people walked past you ten or fifteen would be an spook of some kind. I've probably exaggerated that a bit but it's a hell of a lot. The Colonel knew all about how it worked out here and couldn't be blamed for his line of thought.

There was still doubt in my mind of whether I was doing the right thing. I knew I was more than capable of making MI6 or climbing the ranks of Army Intelligence. Even the SAS would have taken me on for selection and without bragging, I reckon I would have done pretty well there too. All these extra badges and stripes did used to appeal to me, but times were changing. I was starting to think that if I didn't stop climbing ladders soon, I'd be climbing them forever. Ending up never being able to content myself with what I had achieved. I had done almost every course relevant to my trade. On paper I was the ultimate killer. From elicitation techniques to edged weapon training and espionage tradecraft to reflexive fire, with three weeks in Fort Bragg, North Carolina on the Survive Evade Resist and Escape programme thrown in there somewhere. Motorcade operations, critical counter-intelligence high risk rescue and vulnerabilities of an intelligence officer. I could carry on all day but I want to try to avoid boring you if that's at all possible.

Although my letter of resignation had been in for quite a few months I would still question my decision, only on occasion and after thinking about it for a few minutes would always arrive at the same conclusion. I would be taking a hell of a lot away with me when I left the Army. I had been taught things by Britain and America that, as well as costing a fortune were not available to civilians, however special they thought they were. When I left I could go on to learn other things that could only be learnt by being a civilian. Things the Army wouldn't know where to start with. Plus, although I had never been about the money the last few years had cultured me into appreciating the more refined consumables, if you know what I mean. Why not get myself a house and a car? Why not travel first class? I knew I was never in danger of being classed as a snob because I had worked far too hard over the years.

In the Forces you never have to worry about any bills where your food is coming from or where your going to sleep, unless of course you are on Ops but that is different. If I was going to be a civilian I was going to be a rich one. I couldn't be arsed, after all these years of not worrying, getting out to a life of struggling to meet mortgage payments and gas bills. Sure millions of people go through their whole lives working for the cash machine and are probably very decent people because of it. I just couldn't be arsed at almost thirty years old starting the whole process.

In June 97 I had to fly back over to England to go through the motions of being discharged. Handing in kit and signing medical forms and other such things. I thought I would be at least a bit nostalgic about leaving when I saw the DPM again but the feeling never came, not that I can remember anyway. Instead I just wanted to be given a job so I could settle into the planning and get into the whole 'Freelance' scenario. I was asked by various people what my plans where for the future and gave them the old 'I'm gonna go travelling' for a while, see what happens' spiel. I would be told how that sounded very irresponsible at my age and how I should consider that I only had nine years or so left to a full pension. When I look back now it should have been a sad time for me, it was after all the end of an era. This had been my life since leaving school, GCSE's aside the Army had taught me everything I knew. It had taken that teenage 'know it all' streak out of me and given me thirteen years worth of stuff worth knowing. At the time of leaving the Army all I had in my mind was the excitement of working as an enforcer for a superpower in the pursuit of world peace. I admit now I was slightly naive at the time but if I had not have been I might just have ended up staying in the Army and leading a normal happy life.

I had an awful lot of things I had to sort out for the new appointment. Along with being de-mobbed and the daunting prospect of civilian life to deal with there were all sorts of formalities involved in the new professional relationship between myself and Mike. In order to be paid for any work I might undertake I had to open a limited company with an associated bank account in two separate countries. The company was registered in a European country I care not to mention and the account in Nevis in the Caribbean where all income earned outside of Nevis is tax exempt. To avoid chatting noodles to any customs staff I did some research into the Power Cable Industry and the negotiation of maintenance contracts. This itself was a mine field but it was a sort of 'study while you work' set up.

I'm sure however, the in's and out's of setting yourself up as a self-employed murderer wont interest the reader so I'll cut to the chase. I think everyone remembers where they where on August 31st 1997. When I heard the news it was late evening, I was six hours behind GMT. The accident happened around 1215 am and Diana was pronounced dead around 0300. I heard the news in Spanish on a news report whilst sat in my hotel room on Londres, Mexico City. I remember thinking that it couldn't possibly be true and the Mexicans must have the story wrong, when the news report began showing footage and pictures of Diana it came over me like a cold blanket that it really had happened, one of my first thoughts was how on earth did they get to her and why? Again opinions on this story are a book in themselves so let's move on.

Anyone who knows Mexico City will probably be aware that the street parallel with Londres is called Liverpool which I found extremely coincidental to the point where it caused me discomfort, since I set up my own accommodation and saw nothing of the Liverpool street name on any maps. I remember feeling that to miss something like this was a sign that I was already slacking and so I slowed everything right down to get a grip on things again.

The deal with Mike was again pretty simple. I dealt only with him. I had various ways of communicating with him and if for some reason I couldn't then I sat off until I could. I was only just being introduced to the new appointment and I didn't want to jeopardise anything by putting my trust in someone I was unsure of. I never worried about the money I knew that would be there without question as soon as the job was done. The worry lay in getting it right staying alive and making a good impression.

I sat on my balcony drinking room service's pathetic attempt at English tea going over and over it in my head. I knew this was a bad thing to do as you tend to start adding extras and varying your plan in different ways but I did it anyway, probably out of nervousness. Killing someone in close quarters although harder than sniping them from a distance can still be quite easy. The hardest part is the extraction from the kill zone and withdrawal from the country. Planning is everything and providing the execution goes exactly to plan then in theory you should have nothing to worry about.

All I knew about the target was his name what he looked like and where his local was. He was twenty six and whatever it was he had done it had led to the killings of two DEA agents. To hazard a guess I would say knew details of Undercovers and if they didn't shut him up he'd do whatever he did again. I didn't ask and I didn't care. To me he was $80,000 and for anyone so young to be worth this much I could only surmise that in the short spell of him being a man he had worked his way up in his trade at a reasonably fast pace so therefore should be able to take what was coming like the man he thought he was.

I knew what he looked like and where to find him and unless he could do a Sam Beckett and Quantum Leap his way out of Mexico City in the next six hours his life was going to end tonight.

Imagine if you can a reasonably good looking Mexican lad. Add to it an Ali G walk and a boy band image and that's your target. This guy loved himself. He probably sold coke for a living and spent his days cruising round with his 'homey's' listening to rap music. How he had acquired the knowledge of UC's was beyond me, but then I had no idea how far up the food chain he was here in Mexico. What I could be sure of was that the chances of him being alone for any extended period of time were slim. He would also be spending most of his time in crowded places hard to get out of if the shot went off incorrectly.

Crowded places such as night clubs can occasionally prove good places for a job. If you can get the shot off or the knife in without being heard or spotted its possible to put ten or twenty unsuspecting people between yourself and the target before he even hit's the floor. Put a low powered .22 into his liver and the guy will stand there trying to make out the blood on his hand in the flickering night club lights for a good few seconds before he falls to the floor in shock and bleeds to death. The alcohol and fast beating heart from dancing the night away will assist in the bleeding to death but a lot of liver trauma can be treated with simple surgery so lacing the projectile with some form of poison helps. On the other hand if you're spotted by some handbag wielding slapper who starts screaming the whole thing can turn nasty. I decided against the crowded place for now. Nice easy one to start with I thought. I knew all of the theory inside out, at least I knew the theory I had been taught. Finding out how true it all was or if it worked would only come with time. Where the Op was concerned I can't remember if I was nervous or scared. I'm being totally honest here I was one or the other. If you ever meet a person in the same line as work as me and they tell you they weren't one or the other then as far as I'm concerned they are lying, either about their first job or whether they are in the trade at all. Killing a person should not be taken lightly. I think I have already mentioned unless you are completely psychotic there will always be some consideration for what you are doing and the consequences of it. Therefore, although psychopaths would make good serial killers they will never be any good at my job because they would not be concerned with being caught. Fair enough they want to get away with it so they can kill more people but they aren't really that concerned about the consequences. I wanted to get the job done, get out of there alive get paid and never be caught, because I was giving thought to what came after the target hit the floor I couldn't help being the victim of nervousness or fear. I had done all the planning I could; now I had to have faith in myself and keep the nerves at bay until I was well out of the kill zone. If I wanted to break down into a quibbling mess then fine I'd let myself do that. If that is what my body needs to do to get over this first kill then so be it but it wasn't going to happen until the job was done and I was out of Mexico.

The nightclub was a single floor building with its front being around twenty five meters wide with one entrance and two fire escapes at the side and rear of the building.

The road along the side of the building was cluttered with wheelie bins and behind gave a clearing with a short path to the not so busy road to the rear. Night had fallen a while back and the coloured neon lights all over the front of the building lit up the pavement and the door where two very large Mexicans watched the comings and goings of endless party seekers. Music pumped out over the street filling the ears of the passers by as they moved like sheep from one bar to the next. Men in their stylishly creased linen shirts and women in their white mini skirts and skimpy tops.

I sat on a Honda 90 scooter about fifty meters down from the entrance on the opposite side of the road in between two parked cars, casually leaning over the handle bars and drinking from a bottle of lukewarm water. It wasn't hard to blend in, everyone just passed me by without a second look as I sat there like a local, tired from the day's heat and just stopping for a drink on his way home.

You would assume my window of opportunity to be quite small, just the time it took the target to walk from his car to the door and into the club. The night before however he spent a good few minutes doing fancy Fonzy handshakes with the doorman and talking all that shit they talk. The same doorman was on again tonight and I was just hoping they hadn't run out of things to talk about. I was almost guaranteed he would turn up. I had recce'd the place the last two nights and he had been here on both occasions. I had tailed him to his lodgings and other haunts but this was where he did his thing, he was here peddling his drugs more here than he was anywhere else, he was top dog in this club so he'd be here.

My plane left for Fort Worth, Dallas at 6am, I wanted to check in at 4am, it would take an hour to get rid of the scooter and get to the all night spa to wash and change and half an hours taxi drive to the airport. This meant if the bullets were not en route to the target by half past two I had to cancel flights and re-plan. It had just gone ten past one so as yet I had plenty of time.

The snazzy black Ford pick-up rolled up around twenty past one. The back filled with the rest of the Boys R Us clan who were obviously further down the pecking order than the target I thought, due to their seating position. Never the less I knew that probably all of them would be carrying and didn't under estimate them for a second, *even if* every last one of them was hanging over the far side of the vehicle ogling the women.

If I could I wanted to time the kill with the flow of traffic. This wasn't a necessity but it would provide additional cover as I rode off. All the traffic passing the club was slow moving as there would always be some boy racer cruising through at five miles an hour, showing everyone how good his stereo was. I needed to try to get behind a bus or high sided truck that I could over take after the shots were fired to give me cover from any counter-attack.

I waited for the pavement to clear of any obstructive bystanders and pulled out behind a delivery wagon, equivalent in size to a seven and a half tonner. I held back from it about ten meters, so as not to find myself crashing into the back of it at the very moment I didn't want to. I maintained my position in the middle of my side of the road so no one could overtake and leave me blocked in. As I crept along behind the truck towards the kill zone my heart was racing and in all honesty I was nervous as hell. Not of the fact I was about to murder someone but of getting it wrong and having to withdraw under fire with the few rounds I had left in my mag, reloading in front of this lot was not an option. I had no resources nor had I planned to have a full blown fire fight in the middle of Mexico City. Stick to the plan and I'll be fine.

I used a PSS self-loading silent pistol which has an incredibly low sound signature. I could have used a more common silenced pistol as most of the sound from it would have been disguised by the crowd's music and passing vehicles. When I had used this weapon in the past however I had always achieved a high score and good grouping purely because of how comfortable I was with it.

It was small and the 7.62 SP-4 armour piercing steel core rounds where sure to do the job from this range.

The Ford was the target's best chance for cover but he was about five meters from it with his back to me talking to the two doormen. The guys on the truck where focused on the talent to the rear of the vehicle. I was around the seven meter mark when I let off the first round, which hit him smack in the middle of his shoulder blades. His body arched and he fell forward into the doorman who instinctively grabbed him. As I cruised slowly past I fired four more rounds, three of which hit him in various parts of his upper body. By now both doormen where onto the fact that they were under fire and had both attempted to get through the door to the club at the same time dropping the target where he once stood. The sheer size of the fat bastards caused their lunge for cover to prove more difficult than they had hoped and they opted to go for the foetal position instead. As a result the forth round hit the biggest one of the two in his left arm but I didn't mind, the target was down with four rounds in him, I saved one round for the withdrawal should anything else need dropping. The pistol returned to my pocket for now as I twisted back the throttle and overtook the truck in front. None of the lads on the Ford even saw me and the doormen weren't going to look around in a hurry. I whizzed through the traffic passing three streets on my left before turning down the forth. Staying as calm as I could and making sure I stuck to the route, all the time telling myself to stick to the plan as much as I could. I had already gone off the reservation by firing the weapon with my left hand, I had planned to coast past firing with my right then speed off after returning the weapon to my pocket. As it happened, in the final seconds I decided I needed to keep a constant control of the throttle with my right hand so I fired with my left. I was pleased I had in the end as I was away before anyone except the doormen and the target knew I was there. I don't know why I thought it would be better to fire with my right; I was probably just worried about missing.

After taking the forth left I took the next right and slowed right down again before taking the next left and blending back in with the rest of the traffic. Not a single soul thought I was out of place or so much as gave me a second look and yet a few blocks away I had just killed someone. I carried on down to the Parque Americas and parked the scooter up on the pavement. The owner on the other side of town was probably still oblivious to the fact it was missing. I removed the bandana from across my nose and mouth and strolled off on foot back up in the direction of my hotel which I had checked out of earlier. After a half hour walk was the all night spa, where I had dropped off my change of clothes beforehand. It was coming up on 2:30am and I didn't need to leave for the airport until after three.

I got changed into some shorts sat alone in the steam room and allowed the adrenaline to die off. The last hour had been frantic and my whole body was buzzing. I lay there on the wooden bench and went over the job in my head. Asking myself questions like; Where the shots enough to kill him? Did anyone see me? Could anyone have been switched on enough to follow me here? No. I was fine and he was dead, everything had gone really well for a first time.

Well, that was it. I was in the club. I'd made my bones. I didn't feel anything like I thought I would. There wasn't a trace of guilt or worry that I'd get caught. I was confidant and pleased about the job so far. I still had to get rid of the shooter and exit the country but it was all still going to plan. I had envisaged myself thinking about the target. The young Mexican lad, who had his whole life in front of him suddenly having it snatched away by a cold blooded contract killer. Thoughts like this remained absent from my mind though for the time being, I didn't even go as far as thinking about the DEA agents he had killed or the ones I had saved. I didn't give a fuck. I was too busy thinking about how good the shots were from a moving moped with one hand and how the CIA was going to pay me $80,000 for my trouble. I felt like I felt the first time I blew a pheasant out of the sky with my Baikal over and under. I had just stopped something from living and got away with it. I had to keep my head though. I was still in the same country and quite a few miles away from safety. I got washed up and changed and asked the receptionist to bell me a Joey.

I took the taxi to another hotel and asked the driver to drop me just short. I then walked around the block and dropped the clean shooter in a bin and flagged down another cab. Now that I had no sidearm I made damn sure the driver was sincere. Mexico City is probably kidnap capital of the world and it isn't at all uncommon for business men there to flag down a taxi to the airport and never make their flight. I told the driver the exact route to take. The minute he deviated from it my hand was going through his little hatch and with the broken bottle neck I had in my pocket I was going to take as much out of his neck as I could. At this point I didn't care if he was hard of hearing or didn't know his way, I wasn't taking any chances. As it happens the old feller was a genuine guy and we talked about how nice it was for him to pick up a foreigner who had gone to the effort of learning his language and how sick he was of arrogant American businessmen who got annoyed when native Mexicans couldn't speak English. I agreed and we shared a few laughs about why they all chew gum and think they are all jet pilots. The short journey to the airport did a lot to return my adrenaline filled body back to normal and by the time I checked in I myself thought I was a tired power line engineer. I passed through customs relatively easy after they had a mosey through my briefcase to find a load of bullshit proposals and quotations. Six or seven hours later I was eating a chilli cheese taco and drinking freezing beer in my hotel in Texas. Job done. Piece of piss. Get paid. Know mean.

CHAPTER 11

In the afternoon I decided it time to sleep. I hadn't done this for a couple of days again and I was starting to feel it affecting me. After standing in the shower for half an hour and watching a bit of tele I put my head on the pillow and stared at the ceiling for thirty seconds before I closed my eyes. Sure enough he was there waiting for me. Why I thought he wouldn't be I don't know, maybe it was the fact that the last forty eight hours I had been far too busy to think about it in this much depth. During the whole of my planning I hadn't really considered the importance of the fact that this would be my first time. Yes I had been fearful of getting my first job wrong or being caught but the battle of morals hadn't even occurred to me yet. In my planning the young Mexican lad had been nothing but a figure 11 target I had to put rounds in. Amazingly I had coasted through my planning and execution without any hint of remorse, for this I was grateful. I suppose I had to make up for it at some point and sure enough when I closed my eyes the time had come. I seem to remember mentioning earlier that I don't think any decent person could achieve a good night's sleep straight after their first kill and believe it or not I do consider myself a decent person. I'll try and remember to talk more about why later but right now I want it known that for this night at least my conscience did bother me for a while and I'm sure at some point I was talking out loud to the target explaining to him why he had to die by my hand. The same questions presented themselves as they did in Ribnik except this time I had no one to share the guilt with. I had planned and executed this Op on my own. It had gone very well and although I couldn't be one hundred percent certain I was pretty sure it had been successful. The lad didn't stand a chance, for one he didn't even know someone was in town to kill him and secondly he took it in the back so didn't even see it coming. I remembered being punched in the back of the head in a pub in Liverpool, I had no idea of what had happened until I was on the floor. On my way down to the floor I briefly explored the possibilities of what had caused my little trip, has someone accidentally fallen into me or has something from the ceiling just fallen on my head. I hadn't caused any trouble and the lad who got the lucky punch in had simply mistaken me for someone else, all the same when I got back up I wasted half a bottle of Becks on his face before I was ejected by the ever so polite bouncers. The point here is when I felt the smack I didn't have a clue what was going on until I was down, so in a vain attempt to mitigate any guilt I may have been feeling I assumed the guy I had just given the bad news to probably didn't either. My first round looked as though it had gone in through the back of his heart which almost definitely meant his death came as quick as it possibly could. I spent the majority of the night trying to make myself feel better about the whole thing until in the end I just accepted the fact that I had to feel bad about it. I had just murdered a twenty six year old lad and although he deserved to be processed it was still my first kill and the whole taking a life thing isn't as easy to accept as everyone who has never done it seems to think it is. In the morning I reiterated to myself my position in the company and explained to myself how the morning had brought a whole new evolution. The Mexican was filed and I got in touch with Mike to give him the good news.

I didn't have a base as such; I would just hang around in hotels like a travelling salesman waiting for the next job to come up. Mike would always know my whereabouts and all he would ever send was a photograph and a known address, usually by something as simple as

DHL or UPS courier believe it or not. If I needed any extra Intel all I had to do was contact him. The internet and email was up and coming and a lot of hotels had the facility which I occasionally used but only ever in code. I'd make full use of the hotel's gyms to maintain my fitness and spend my abundance of free time reading books that could improve my service.

Between September 97 and July 98 the jobs came in thick and fast. I'd follow the breadcrumbs to the job carry it out and withdraw to a safe country to live it up and wait for the next job. I favoured the States as a rule as I was able to have a face to face with Mike so we could de-brief each other. Some of the time I was out of the kill zone so fast I wouldn't know if I'd been successful or not until I met up with Mike. Along with the States I'd stay in Monaco and Tenerife I didn't once return home.

By the summer of 1998 I had amassed $900,000. The jobs varied in price but averaged around a hundred and twenty grand. My work had taken me to Cyprus, Egypt Thailand and a whole host of other 'not very legally lenient' countries. In eleven months I killed six men and one woman, six with firearms and one with a blade. I didn't once stop to think further than continuing to improve my skills and make more money. I didn't even ask what most of them had done to get themselves processed I just went to work each day and made people die.

On a trip to Washington I bumped into Mike and Lauren at the Reflection Pool. I was there to see him but not at that exact time. As I greeted him Mike looked like he had seen a ghost, his face went white and his body language was extremely defensive. I put my hand onto Lauren's hair and said hello. Before she could reply Mike told her to go and play so we could talk grown up stuff. As she walked away I asked mike what was wrong. He told me there wasn't anything wrong, we just couldn't talk business while Lauren was around. I agreed and told him to leave the job talk until our arranged meeting later on.

"Are you sure that's all that's wrong mate? You look worried about something!" I said.

"Yeah of course, I'm just having some family time and didn't expect to see you that's all." He replied.

"That's all I need to hear mate, you carry on I'll see you later."

"I'm not being funny or anything pal." He shouted as I walked off.

"I know mate, I'll leave ya to it. See ya later." I shouted.

When I returned to me hotel room I felt like you used to feel as a kid. Stood outside the headmaster's office before a bollocking. My stomach was upside down and I felt like I had somehow abused Lauren. I knew what Mike's problem was, he didn't want a murderer near his daughter. I couldn't blame him but for one I was on his side and secondly he was the one pushing the buttons I just pulled the trigger. At first I though of him as a cheeky bastard. Who the fuck was he to call me a murderer? He had taken lives and all my jobs had been organised and sanctioned by him. After a bit of open minded thinking I went on to look at it from his angle. For all he knew I could have taken him or even Lauren on as a job for somebody else. I would never have done this for any amount of money but how would he know this? We hadn't seen enough of each other over the last year for him to be sure.

Really I was just telling myself this to make me feel better. I had hoped he could trust me more than he did, especially where his family where concerned. I had always looked on them as family of my own and I needed him to know this. Whatever we had to talk about tonight this took priority. I needed it sorting. I wouldn't know what someone who had been wrongly accused of being a paedophile feels like but I was pretty sure I was feeling something similar. I was sick at the thought of him thinking I could blow a whole in his baby girl or cut her throat. The thoughts of these actions started staining my mind. What had he done? I was so angry. I hadn't felt anger towards anyone for years and I certainly felt it now. I loved watching that girl play. I hadn't seen much of her in the last year fair enough but even so I wouldn't think twice about dying to keep her safe. Now I was having thoughts of harming her. In no way were they intentions but the amounts of deaths I had caused in the last year mixed with Mike's feelings were causing some pretty nasty visions in my mind. I couldn't wait to talk about this with him. I had to clear this up.

We met at nine in the lobby of the usual hotel and sat in the big couches tucked away in a corner near the bar. I asked if he wanted a drink and he said something like;

"Do ducks float?"

"Sit down I'll go the bar, can't be arsed waitin for the fuckin waitress." I said.

A couple of minutes later I returned with two bottles of Coors.

"You made me feel like shit before." I said, calmly.

"Hey, no offence meant mate but hit men aren't the type of company I had in mind for my daughter. If you don't like it tough shit." he said, firmly.

"Thanks a lot mate, do you really think I would ever harm her, or the rest of your family for that matter?"

"I know you would never harm her mate I didn't mean that. Its just not good company for her. Your traits will come out around her how ever deep you bury them and I just don't want her round that. Don't take offence mate please."

"So do your traits come out around her then?" I replied.

"I'm her dad." he snapped.

"Your not going to win this argument mate." I said. "You once told me people like you and me were necessary to protect people like Lauren and Hailey."

"I know, but not at close quarters. I'd buy a Doberman to guard my garden not Lauren's bed."

"Let me tell you something about me." I said to him, moving forward to the edge of my seat. "When I was a kid I loved my mum and dad so I know I'm capable of the emotion whatever you think I am. I've been learning to kill people since I left school and killing them, for you, for the last year. I'm good at it I know, maybe too good at it because it's started to make my only real friend scared of me."

"Arrrrgh hang on a minute." He attempted to interrupt.

"No you hang on." I snapped. "I love Lauren and I love you wife too."

"You love my wife?" He tried to soften the whole thing with a joke but it was too late.

"Fuck off I'm serious." I shouted, drawing attention from the bar. I lowered my voice and continued.

"I don't have much room in my heart for love because the more lives I end the colder it gets but let me tell you this, I would die protecting you and you family and you better fukin remember it. I've got almost a million dollars to my name now, so that's what *I'm* worth. If I had a hundred million I wouldn't even be close to being worth what your family is to me. So I'd go first believe me."

"Hailey has cancer." He interrupted. I could have gone on for another ten minutes or so with this totally unrehearsed speech but that stopped me in my tracks.

"What?" I knew what he had said but 'what' was all I could think of saying.

"She has breast and bone cancer so she'll probably be going first mate." He said, looking me in the eye.

I didn't know what to say to him so I just sat back in my seat. Not everyone dies of cancer of course but in our case Hailey's had spread beyond help. The tests radiotherapy and chemotherapy had been going on for a while and although in my little world I thought I was entitled to know, they had kept it from me for whatever reasons. I hadn't actually seen Hailey for some time but we spoke often on the phone and she always talked to me like a good friend. I suppose, thinking about it now I considered Mike and his family to be closer to me than I *thought* they actually felt they were. Until our heart to heart tonight I'd never actually told Mike how good a friend he was or why. We had just done what we do and laughed and joked our way into a good friendship. Mike had always felt the same but also had never felt it necessary to tell me about it. I'm sure it's the same for other blokes. As pathetic as it may sound, men find it awkward to tell another man how much he thinks of him, probably for fear of being mistaken as gay. It was unfortunate we should need a situation such as Hailey's to bring it out of us.

If the growth rate of the cancer stayed as it was, the doctors estimated her to have as much as two or three years left. We talked about the whole thing until late again and around twelve Mike told me he had better get back to her. Usually he would have told me he wanted to watch the NFL highlights or some manly shit like that but the bond between us had been brought to light tonight and when we went our separate ways we were much closer friends than we were earlier.

Back in my hotel room I sat on the end of my bed and stared at the waste paper basket for over an hour. I only changed position to ease the ache that had appeared in my back from slouching for so long. Lay on my back with my legs on the floor I re-directed my vacant gaze to the ceiling. Everything I had ever done was flashing through my mind like a strobe light. All the bad people myself and Mike had processed and this is the thanks we get. We take all that evil from the world by becoming it ourselves and our reward is to lose someone we love.

I explored all avenues of course, feeling I had done the world a favour and not been thanked properly soon changed to feeling Mike and myself had got what we deserved. Who did we think we were deciding who should live and who should die? Had Death himself decided to let us know that he had no need for employees and could do just fine on his own? Maybe it was just Hailey's time to be processed and that was how I should look at it. I had after all adopted this view every time I had processed an unknown. Just because I didn't know them didn't mean there wasn't someone who did, who would get upset at their death. I could never sell that view to Mike though; he had been blinded by emotional pain. I thought I was upset by it all. What must he have been feeling? His perfect family had been shattered by an unknown force that had made the decision that Hailey should die slowly over the next three years. He didn't care about theories from anyone else, he had his own and whatever it was, he would die with it. He told me later that he thought it was punishment for what he had done, he thought that God was making damn sure Mike knew that he was pissed off with him for interfering with his plans. I never once told him I thought it was all bollocks; I just tried to comfort him as best I could. He had his faith and if that was how he dealt with it then I wasn't going to take any of that away from him. He will probably be needing it after Hailey had been,… had died.

He went through a spell of feeling guilty for trying to keep me away from Lauren that day at the Reflection Pool. He told me how he never meant any of the things he had said about me that night and blamed it all on how he was finding the whole thing so difficult. He worried that after Hailey was gone, Lauren would be all he had left and he needed to at least attempt to hide her from the eyes of death whatever form he took. Without disrespecting him Mike was on his way out. The whole situation with Hailey and Lauren had made him soft, which at his time of life was not a bad thing but if he wasn't careful it could push him over the edge.

Christmas approached and although there was a chance this could have been their last together as a family I was still asked to spend it with them. Field work stopped for the time being and although Mike had to go into the office most days nothing about either of our lives involved the dark side of the job.

Lauren was in my life everyday for three weeks and she came to mean a lot to me. At the same time I maintained a hard shell. Mike had lost it a few times in front of me and although I had said how sad I thought the whole thing was I had not yet shown any effect of it in front of any of them. I would question whether maintaining this image was the correct thing to do. Should I remain an unaffected pillar of strength for them all or might this give the impression I don't love them enough to care. I think Mike secretly knew my position and just kept quiet about it.

Lauren came to trust me in no time, now nine she was full of cuddles for everyone especially me for some reason. Probably because she could sense the pain in her mum and dad, with me it was buried deep and I would just laugh and play with her as often as she liked.

She cried the day I left for Britain. It was the end of January 99, I felt that what they were going through they had to now face without me there. It was starting to come to a head. Hailey was looking really ill and Lauren now knew that it was more than just the illness Mike and Hailey had been telling her it was. Although I was good help to them by taking Lauren off their hands when they needed time together I felt I was in the way of a very important milestone in her life. She was about to lose her mum and this needed to be explained to her so they could spend their last few months together as a family.

I came home to Liverpool and through my limited company bought a house in West Derby. My days were spent making myself meals maintaining my fitness and driving in and out of town in my new Range Rover buying shit. I would often feel like I had abandoned my only friend and his family in their hour of need but as painful as it was for me I knew I had done the right thing. I just hoped if and when I saw Lauren again she would understand why I left. As hard I thought I was, I missed her.

CHAPTER 12

Mike knew my reasons for leaving as did Hailey; at least they had their own idea of what my reasons were. Whatever they thought they knew I wasn't doing it as a kop out. I stayed in touch with Hailey through the occasional phone call and of course Mike through work. I operated from West Derby flying all over the miserable planet sorting out problems the CIA and NSA had come across during phone calls about trade disputes or meetings concerning the importation of contraband. The money piled up in Nevis as did the bodies in the morgue and I got better and better at what I did. By the beginning of my third year working for Mike I had processed fourteen people and earned over two and a half million dollars. I had filled my home with expensive tele's furniture and nice cars, I thought nothing of flying over to the states first class on a Friday morning for the weekend so I could go down to the gun club to keep my skills up. I had become a consumer, the one thing I thought I would always avoid becoming. I think I did the whole rich life thing to justify what I was doing. This bit is kind of hard to explain.

Since Bosnia I had made it my life mission to be as good as I could be at ending lives and I had the found a way of selling my skills at a reasonably high price. Along the way I had met a family which despite my remorseless approach to life had come to mean a lot to me. This family was about to be torn apart by death, and I suppose I was meant to be feeling as though my actions had caused this through some sort of karma. I didn't think like this though. This approach to life was way beyond me. Instead I accepted it by making the whole thing as simple as I could. Death happened whether I liked it or not or whether I dealt it or not. Hailey was on her way out regardless of what I had done or could do. I was still making tens of thousands of dollars for taking lives so I might as well be spending it. Letting it all build up in a bank account then being processed myself would have made the whole thing a waste of time. Right?

My Uncle Jeff and Aunty Pauline were under the impression I worked for an American based dot com company that was cashing in on the internet craze. Still as proud as ever they would call round on occasion to see their rich nephew who had a detached house in West

Derby and one of those new Range Rovers, living life to the full and loving every minute of it.

Truth be known I was lost. I was trapped in the rat race just like the city workers but instead of selling stocks and shares to the investors I was selling death to the CIA. I didn't know how to get out or even if I wanted to, I just kept on going. I thought about Lauren and how she might view death now she knew of her mum's illness. Would she manage to perceive it as simplistically as me and even if she could would this make losing her mum any easier to take? I pictured her in her pink pyjamas bringing me the beer back from the fridge, back when her life was filled with sweets toys and a healthy mum. What must her life be like now? I bet the sweets didn't taste the same nor the toys hold the same meaning anymore, she probably just sat wanting to know why mummy had to go to heaven. I would bet my house she had asked Mike that very question. I'd have loved to hear his answer.

I thought about the job in Jacobs and how the simple life seemed so much more appealing. I would probably have long settled down by now with my own son or daughter. I'd have never known Lauren or Mike and Hailey and I'd have not killed fourteen people, who since leaving Lauren had been in my dreams calling out to me. Not since the night in Texas had I had a sleepless night because of the job until I left Lauren. Now I would dream of her being harmed, sometimes by the people I had killed and sometimes by myself. The dreams were so disturbing I would wake sometimes in a cold sweat and cry out. I could feel myself going soft. I went over all the turning points in my life every night a thousand times; Lime Street, Ribnik Walton Park duck pond and Mexico City. What if I'd done this? What if I'd done that? I was convinced I was having a breakdown of some kind. As hard as I tried I couldn't get a grip.

I couldn't figure out why I had become so attached to Lauren, she was after all just my mates daughter. I'd think about it a lot and one conclusion I arrived at was that after the cancer I saw her as scared innocence trapped in between two aspects of death. The giver of it and the receiver of it. I longed for her to be as far away from it as possible. Of course she didn't know about her dad's job but never the less death surrounded her. I wished I hadn't had chosen my path so I could shelter her from it but if I hadn't I'd never have known her. I thought about Mike and how, if he was thinking the same thing how it must be tearing him apart. He would blame himself for the rest of his days for Hailey's death and how would that affect Lauren?

1999 and Millennium was a very lonely time for me. I'd never had a problem being alone, I always had been. Since I had started to break though things were different.

I knew I was going soft and in a way I didn't want to stop it. The people I had killed were all people who had been the cause of harm to others, so not once was I sorry for turning them off. I just wished that now Lauren needed comfort from death I could wipe the slate clean of all the deaths her dad had ever caused so he could keep it together for her. I would gladly take on his nightmares for him if he had any. If he didn't then I wished I could have a clean slate for her. I just didn't want her around death, 'whatever form it took'.

Mike's plan was to take retirement so he could spend the last few months with Hailey and make some plans for his and Lauren's future. Of course this is only what anyone in Mike's situation would do, but then not everyone in Mike's situation is a Field Ops Planner for the CIA. He had loose ends to tie up and assets to hand over to his replacement.

He asked me if I wanted to continue with the jobs. This was a bigger decision than it sounds. I had known Mike for years now and he was the only form of contact I had with the American Government. I'm pretty sure there was a file on me somewhere in Langley but no one would have ever been interested while Mike was controlling everything perfectly. The new guy however may be totally different, he might be the type to shout my name all over Capitol Hill and not give a shit about the consequences. I had enough money now to retire on, sure I would have to draw my horns in slightly but I had no problem with that. I could maybe move out to the States and help Mike with Lauren, live out my days fishing or some shit like that.

I do know the reason why I decided to take a risk with some more jobs but every time I go over it in my head I feel more and more stupid. I was worried about waking up each day and having nothing to plan or train for. Not having drills and daily routines to keep me living my life instead of sitting back and simply waiting to die. I couldn't bare the thought of lying in bed until ten in the morning then sitting in my boxie's all day having my brain melted by daytime television. It was a big risk to take and although I told myself I was too good to be caught out I knew somewhere in the back of my head that someone can always get to you if they have the bottle.

The new lad was called Keiron. I didn't get to know as much about him as I would have liked but then I wasn't going to be working with him too long.

On March the 13th 2000 at two thirty in the morning a thickset tough as nails ex Marine fell gently sideways to find support on the lime green plasterboard wall. His only comfort was a ten year old girl who clung desperately tight to his waist as he pulled her head tighter to him to absorb her tears in his unlaundered sweatshirt.

Why is it that when people hear or deliver news of a death they say sorry? Mike had left Hailey's bed side at the hospital to come home for Lauren who was crying for her mum. I had fell asleep in a chair next to her bed when she woke me around half past one. "Is Mummy still ok?" she asked me. She told me how she had dreamt of Hailey sailing away on a big white ship waving to her. Lauren was crying for her to come back but the boat couldn't because the wind was blowing the wrong way. I made the mistake of saying Hailey was ok and Mike was asleep next to her bed just like I was for Lauren. She cried for him and her mum to come home so much that I had to ring him. I could usually calm her but tonight was different, as if she knew it was her mum's last night.

Mike was in the house barely five minutes when his phone rang, the piercing tone of the trademark Nokia tune still haunts me to this day. As it rang we exchanged looks of fear as we expected the worst. I stood holding Lauren's hand in the light of the open fridge as she put back the milk carton she had just drank from. Mike said very little on the phone, when he said OK Lauren and I knew what had happened. "Has Mummy left now Daddy?" she asked. "Yeah baby she has." Mike replied as his voice broke to begin crying. Lauren pulled from my hand and ran across the marble floor in her fluffy slippers towards her dad. He fell gently against the wall as if the sadness he felt had stopped his body from supporting itself. His daughter clung to his waist Mike put his hands around her head as they both cried. I looked into the fridge and stared for what seemed like an eternity at a half eaten bag of Hershey's chocolates. I thought about where Hailey might be right at that moment. Was she with us right there in the kitchen? Did she now know what myself and Mike had been doing for a living? Was she mad at us? What if I had been wrong all these years, thinking that life ends with death? What if there was a spirit world or even a heaven? This soon passed though and I returned to thinking about Lauren and Mike. After two solid hours crying Mike took Lauren to bed. I think she actually cried herself to sleep about five o'clock. Mike lay there next to her restless for the rest of the morning. In the afternoon Lauren and Mike sat in different parts of the house staring into space probably both not knowing what happens next. I sat in the kitchen racking my brains for lines to reassure or comfort them both. There really isn't any, none that I could think of anyway. I made tea for them both and cut Laurens meat up into little pieces for her like I would when she was little. It was always something she loved me doing because I would make all the pieces exactly the same size then eat the edges myself so there weren't any odd sized pieces. It was a running gag between us and she would always smile when I did it. Not

129

today though. Today she just stared at her plate eyes red and nose blocked from crying. I stood at the kitchen sink and looked out the window as I left them to stare at their food in peace. There was going to be a lot to sort out over the next few days and as much as I was willing to do it all I didn't know how to tell Mike I would. He wasn't going to let me any how, it was something he felt he had to do. He did ask that I stay to help out with Lauren though which I was more than happy to do.

At the funeral Lauren told me that if I was sad and needed someone to cuddle I could cuddle her. Although I didn't actually spill tears this was the closest I had come to crying since I was a kid. All the pain and sadness she must have been feeling and she still found it in her heart to offer *me* of all people a shoulder to cry on. I wanted her to feel that her help was needed so I took her up on her offer. I still tell myself that I did it for her and I really am convinced I did, but for some reason in the back of my mind a voice tells me that a lot of that cuddle was for me.

CHAPTER 13

Mike took compassionate leave to look after Lauren leading up to his retirement and the handover of me to Keiron took place during my stay in Washington. My track record with Mike was enough for Keiron to base his judgements on. He told Mike he wanted a meet but I insisted not. There wasn't any need for him to know what I looked like. I was there to be used as needed and if he wasn't happy with my terms then I would walk away. He knew how valuable I was to his cause and after a bit of sulking he came round to my way of thinking. However I still considered my location to be uncomfortably close to Keiron and knew that I couldn't continue to stay in Washington for much longer. Laurens summer break from school was coming up and I suggested to Mike that it may be a good idea if the two of them come visit Liverpool for a while. My house was easily big enough for us all to have our own privacy.

Mike was quite open about the fact that he thought it would be a bad idea for him to let Lauren stay in my house while I was still active. He was right of course, what if one of my targets had an acquaintance who tracked me down or Keiron changed his mind about employing me. We explored all options and came to the conclusion that Mike could just as easily be tracked down in Washington now that his protection from the CIA would be limited. The aftercare program offered to its former employees is not one of the agency's selling points so we decided we could offer Lauren more protection if we stayed together, at least for the time being. Plus my house was like a fortress and as far as I knew no one in the CIA knew were it was.

It was decided then, Lauren was coming to Liverpool. Naturally she was overwhelmed with excitement as she wasn't exactly well travelled. Considering Hailey had only been gone three months Lauren was taking it surprisingly well. She would still cry quite a lot and have quiet days but most of the time she was reasonably high spirited considering her situation.

The over night flight from Dulles was an adventure for Lauren, it was her first time on a plane and she flew first class. Not bad hey. After take off she made herself comfy with her complimentary quilt and pillow and only woke up for her meal and to watch a bit of tele before dosing off again. I did my best to take Mike's mind off things but despite my efforts the conversation always seemed to drift back to Hailey. He told me that Lauren had told him she was scared she would forget what 'mummy' looked like. I could feel comments like that beginning to cut through my callous exterior and have an effect on me. It was by no means a serious effect but certainly a noticeable one. In the past I wouldn't have been phased at all by someone else's sadness, even Laurens. Now though I was beginning to feel it. Getting to know this family had caused me to start caring about them. I had never really got to know anyone else and by keeping everyone at arms length I had managed to avoid being slowed down by emotion. My feelings for this family were definitely growing and I started to think that maybe I had made a mistake by telling Keiron I would continue working for him. I set myself certain targets to try and ease the fact that really I had fucked up and should have quit while I was ahead. I was thirty three now and I told myself that by thirty six I wanted to be out of the game and have enough money to live out my days carefree with plenty of holidays a nice car and an Everton season ticket. Not much to ask right?

In August 2000 I left Lauren and Mike in West Derby and headed for Pakistan. Pakistan is not one of the friendliest places on the planet and if was caught over there as an assassin I think it would be safe to say I wouldn't be heard of again. With this in mind I decided to tell Keiron that the one hundred grand he had set aside for me needed to be increased to one fifty. The financial value of the jobs was now very much a contributing factor to my level of motivation. It was no longer about the thrill or the skill it was about how much money I could make in the next three years so I could retire as planned and spend more time with Lauren.

The Committee to Protect Journalists was founded in 1981 to protect organisations and individuals in the news game. It didn't take into account their nationalities or ideologies just their protection, so they could report on world events. I'm not saying I was working for them on this occasion just mentioning that I thought they might have had an involvement. The name of the target isn't important though I can discuss in limited detail why he had to leave us.

For the purpose of the story the target will be called Afzal. His age was unconfirmed as forty six years, he was only of slight build and had no wife or children that we knew of. In no way should he be considered a terrorist. This man was far too selfish to devote himself to any cause other than his own. Although he was motivated purely by money he did not have a considerable amount as most of the money he made from his activities was quickly squandered. He had a brother who was married with three children and from our Intel it was clear that emotionally he was close enough to them for them to be used as leverage if need be.

Afzal's area of employment was kidnapping but since he did not have the balls or the contacts to negotiate ransom demands with foreign governments he would offer his skills out at a reasonably low price to terrorist organisations and splinter cells. His methods were mostly smash and grab and although crude took a certain amount of skill and planning. Where Journalists were concerned there would usually be some form of close protection involved, be it private bodyguards the police or army. He had only snatched two people that we knew of both of which were Indian journalists reporting of the situation in Kashmir. Indian reporters are about as welcome in Pakistan as Safestyle window salesmen are in my living room and the two of them were killed after ransom demands were not even viewed let alone discussed or agreed to.

Afzal's employers had begun to make it quite clear that the kidnapping of foreign reporters was to become more and more common over the coming years and when US reporter David Smyth's bodyguard was killed in a unsuccessful kidnap attempt by Afzal's gang my employers thought it time to send a message.

David Smyth was a reporter for a well known New York based news group. As well as being very good at his job and having balls as big water melons he was also considered very important by the CIA. If they were to ever need something to make headline news, whether it be to calm a local or national panic or even to create one they could usually bank on Smyth to do this for them. He could do this not only because his work was so well respected but because Smyth and his editor were in each others pockets, some people thought literally.

Losing Smyth was not an option, he would prove too difficult to replace and if solving the problem was only going to cost them a hundred and fifty grand, well, its Asda price!

Whatever we decided Smyth needed to be able to stay in Pakistan. His work there was important to America's bigger picture and extracting him from the country was another option unavailable to us.

This meant two things; if we kill Afzal we remove the possibility of another snatch attempt on Smyth. However, if we do remove the Afzal threat how long will it be before someone takes his place and goes for Smyth anyway? Then someone suggested we leave Afzal doing what he was doing but send him a clear message that Smyth was one reporter not to be bothered again. This seemed the best option, for now anyway. It couldn't hurt to test the water, if he doesn't get the message we return to plan A and take him out. Smyth would be under close protection for the duration of the Op so at worst it would cost us a few extra quid on explosives. I was on a price job not piece work which meant I got paid for achieving the original result not for how many people I processed, the original result being Smyth's future safety.

So what form should our message to Afzal take? If we killed his brother or his nieces and nephews then he might adopt the 'nothing to lose' attitude and go off the rails completely and the last thing we needed was a time bomb psychopath on our hands. His sister-in-law was a safer option. Although Afzal was close to her the psychologist involved insisted this was the best way for us to express our sincerity to him yet keep him from going bananas and taking it out on other US civilians. He had to know that the attack on her was because of his attempt on Smyth so if he was going to flip he would almost certainly go for Smyth again. According to the shrink it would be in Afzal's best interests to cry quietly about the whole thing and thank his god we stopped at his sister-in-law. Despite his links with the terrorist groups he would not be able to do anything quick enough to stop me getting to him and his brother should he wish to pursue a revenge attack.

I sat at the back of the briefing room in the American Embassy in Islamabad not uttering a single word. I had never seen any member of the planning team here as they had never seen me and hopefully I would never be seeing any of them again. Keiron had informed them of my arrival and my identification took place by way of a series of verbal identification techniques. I knew my face would now be on the CCTV at the Embassy but them knowing what I looked like was not as concerning to me as I originally made it sound. It was Keiron I wanted to avoid letting know what to look for in case I needed this advantage at a later date.

I was not included in the decision making at all. In the opinion of the planning team I was a tool sat in the corner waiting to be put to use. I was allowed to sit in for the majority of the discussions so I could learn the Intel on the targets to get as good a head start as I could on my target profiles. These are of course necessary to me so I can learn of habits and routines to make the job as smooth as possible.

Despite the fact that the other three people in the room were talking about executing women and children I still got the feeling that they thought I was somehow more unacceptable than them. It could just have been because I was the outsider and the other three worked together from day to day, though somehow I felt it was more than that. I could feel their eyes on me while I looked away as if they were looking at me and asking themselves, how I could kill people as easily as I did? The psychologist especially, she was around forty five to fifty and tried her hardest to use her facial expressions to show the rest of us that deep down she was really opposed to what we were doing. I think she must have forgotten that it was her who made the suggestion of killing his sister-in-law. I got the impression that the three of them thought it was all just a big game and after a night of saying who should be killed could go to bed and wake in the morning with everything fixed. The people they had chosen to be removed from the picture hadn't really had their throats slashed or their heads blown off, they just weren't there anymore. I assume they were looking at me in disgust to attempt to remove any guilt they might have been feeling, they decided who died I just made them die. We were both as bad or as good as each other and what ever credit or blame I was going to take for my actions they were going to share with me.

Peshawar is roughly two hundred kilometres west of Islamabad. Imagine if you can a wild west town in the east, men in baggy trousers and long loose shirts with bullet studded bandoleers across there chests and firearms at their side. During weddings or other such celebrations the streets would be filled with wild cheers and the occasional salvo of gun fire. The town and surrounding areas are full of spectacular architecture with museums library's and university's all part of the picture. Peshawar is surrounded by high walls with probably close to twenty entry gates. The scattered parks and lawns some how reminded me that this was once a colony and the Lords or Governors in charge here had clearly wanted a touch of home at hand. A lot of Peshawar's surrounding areas are still under the jurisdiction of tribal law and many places cannot be visited without a permit. The majority of Pathan men carry firearms and are far from worried about using it should you rub them up the wrong way. This doesn't mean that anyone can walk around with a gun at their side, if I had have set foot in that place with my Glock tucked down my belt I wouldn't have made any friends in a hurry. The Pashtun tribe live by the three concepts of Pashtunwali, revenge respect and hospitality. The guys here are the type to die for their honour without giving it a second thought and at the same time will give shelter to their sworn enemy should he ask for it. Their lack of western inconsequential comforts like sky TV and smoothie makers has kept them fully aware of the importance of life's basic prerequisites. Good manners confidence hard work and above all the will and ability to fight to the death in the name of self preservation. In short these blokes were hard as fuck but would pull out all the stops to make you feel welcome. For the record it was the Pashtuns who brought us the Mujaheddin.

Shabby was no different. Short for his second name Shahabad 'Shabby' also gave a very good description of his appearance. He was probably fifty odd and spoke better

English than I did, although he did struggle sometimes to understand my accent which he called Libberpoo. He was assigned as my guide by someone I had no reason to trust at the Embassy. I had no choice though, I couldn't speak any of the languages they spoke here and although I could quite easily find my way around with a map and compass I wasn't completely aware of where I could and couldn't go without a native. I couldn't complete the whole Op being completely hidden so I needed someone to get me past the suspicious eyes. I didn't have time to start interviewing locals for the post so like I said I had no choice but to trust him, I just had to make sure I kept an eye on him at all times. As it turned out he was a sound bloke, loyal to the cause of peace and quite willing to help us in whatever methods we followed in pursuit of this goal, without asking any questions. What he was told was of course very limited but he did have to know I wasn't the press photographer I was pretending to be in case he dropped me in it with the local authorities.

He drove the pair of us round in a 1959 series two Landrover and carried all my photo gear for me. Anything I needed he could get me, including my tools as and when I needed them. The job itself was easy but I had been given a fortnight so I wanted it done right. The research had to be as extensive as it would any other job. Again the most important part of the job wasn't ending the sister-in-laws life it was getting out of the country alive.

All my permits were sorted by the Embassy who also went out of their way to make sure it wasn't at all apparent that it had been sorted by them. After I left Islamabad for Peshawar there was no running back to them should I be caught as an intruder or assassin, I was on my own, I had no doubt that Shabby had his own escape plan and would be nowhere to be seen should the shit hit the fan. I had three flights booked in three different names at five day intervals. My passports and tickets where being held in safe deposit boxes at the Marriot Hotel in Islamabad. That was as detailed as my escape plan got. There weren't many other options available to me being that I wanted help from as fewer people as possible. Hiking out of there was not an option I wanted to consider, with K2 to the north and the Khyber Pass to the west it wasn't exactly likely to compare to a stroll around Derwent water, getting back to an airport and on a plane before any alarms were raised was a must.

CHAPTER 14

I have always considered myself well travelled and cultured, even back during my time in Pakistan I felt as though I could handle any environment. The Karkhano market though was something else. I don't think there is a bloke alive who can handle women and shops when they are put near each other. People of all ages and sex would be at there stalls selling everything from flour to western porn. Giant wooden and clay bowls would litter the passage ways filled with an array of brightly coloured beans herbs and spices. The odd canvas would protect the shoppers from the heat of the burning sun as well as keep the fruit and veg from shrivelling up. Horse trading in the 'City of Flowers' is rife. Horses and donkeys are as much part of life here as cars and bikes are in Britain. The Friday horse market would be packed with buyers and sellers of mostly Afghan horses. During the war in Afghanistan thousands of wild horses fled to Pakistan were they have since been rounded up by Pakistani horse traders and are sold back to the Afghans at sometimes as much as thirty thousand rupees. The smells sights and sounds experienced whilst walking through one of the Karkhano's many passage ways grab you tightly and pull you without resistance into their world. It's almost as if the section of market you are in becomes cocooned in a thick invisible layer of culture preventing any escape back to the world you know. The traders can be very intimidating to the visitor and tourists that venture this far north usually find themselves paying ten times what they needed to just to get themselves away from the overpowering merchants.

I had been at the market since seven AM; the sister-in-law would come here most days to gather whatever she needed for her family. Shabby was tailing her from her primitive accommodation to the market in order for me to be able to get a fix on her as she arrived. Both of us tailing her in was an unnecessary risk of being compromised. As her bus arrived Shabby could point her out to me from a distance and retire out of sight. Identifying her otherwise would prove to be a problem since Muslim women hide their faces most of the time.

Shabby made me aware of her by standing behind her right shoulder and raising his right hand to his forehead then walked off in the opposite direction and waiting a moment to check I tailed the right one. I followed as she moved gracefully from stall to stall bartering and buying what she needed. I could easily fit in as a local with my dark thick hair and olive skin but I decided it best not to try too hard to deceive. It would be better for me to take my chances as a western photographer than pretend to be a Pakistani who couldn't speak a word of his own language. Plus looking like a photographer and carrying all the gear round with me I could get away with taking the odd snap or two of the target in case I did need them for any part of the planning.

From this first day of researching her I could tell something wasn't right. Something about her told me she wasn't a valid target. I had been killing people long enough now to know that her body language her manner and the expressions from the people she was interacting with were not those of someone who I would feel comfortable about killing. I know I was at a distance and it was early days yet but from day one something about this job made me feel perturbed.

I logged her habits just the same though and it wasn't long before I felt I had enough. I didn't need to tail her home, not today anyway. I took my findings, which of course were jotted down on nothing more than parts of my brain and returned to my guest house to start my planning. My accommodation was as primitive as it came, the dry hot air in there made it virtually impossible to get any rest. I only had to be in the room five minutes or so and every item of clothing I had on would be welded to my skin. There was an old battered table and chair at the window and a fake flower in a plastic jar next to the single bed. The view was that of section of the city wall, which I probably could have reached across and touched despite the fact there was supposed to be a road in between my building and the wall. The street below was cluttered with people bikes and donkeys which managed to kick up enough dust on passing to send it straight through my bedroom window and into my lungs while I tried to sleep. Without being offensive I hated the place, hot dirty and more to the point too many thousand miles away from home which lately I had started missing when I left it.

I layback on the wok shaped bed and reflected on the day. I couldn't help thinking how wrong it would be to kill this woman. Of course I couldn't be certain but something told me that she had never put a foot wrong in her life. The way she treated the strangers at the market alone was enough to convince me. The mental impression I built of her in my head was one of a hard working loving mother who lived only for her family. Market in the morning, then home to cook and clean for her children and husband, regardless of how much of a dick he was. Mike at this point would be going on about how I had fallen for her and wanted to marry her and not murder her but it wasn't like that. Yes I agree I might have been going soft since all the goings on with Lauren, I'm not ashamed to admit it now but it certainly wasn't me falling for this woman. My portfolio had a certain pattern to it and that is that everyone I had processed over the years had done something to warrant their demise and my turning them off benefited a great deal of people. This time was not going to benefit anyone. No matter what I did I couldn't justify the life to death ratio between this woman and an American reporter. This girl won't have even known if or why this man existed let alone have anything to do with his attempted kidnapping. This was a classic case of wrong place at wrong time and I wasn't going to be the one to end her life. Mike would never have sent me to do a job like this, everything was very quickly turning to shit and even more so now I wished I'd quit at the same time as Mike. I had already made the decision to abort, that took all of five minutes and was the easy part, now I had to get out of the country before my employers found out and pulled the plug.

It was 9pm, Shabby would be here at 7am again which meant I had ten hours to get clear. I didn't know what sort of surveillance the Americans had on me but I had convinced myself they would have pinned some sort of tail on me or would be monitoring my exit route. This meant the airports would be a bad idea. All they had to do was inform the authorities I was a spy or contract killer and the Pakistani Police and Army would do the rest of their job for them. If the alarm was raised at the airport I would have very little chance of escape. I didn't want to go back for my passports either, there was very little chance they knew where I had stashed them but a little chance was enough to deter me. If I was spotted at the hotel and they knew my passports where there then there was only really one conclusion they would come to. I had one passport on me along with my permit to roam the territories and one emergency back up passport I had sewn into the lining of my pack. I would just have to take my chances with these.

I sat on my small balcony and surveyed the street below for any out of place looking people. I didn't really think they would be down there watching me all night but I had to check. It was probably more likely the case that Shabby was keeping tabs on me and had been told to report anything out of the ordinary in my day to day activities. Once he knew I was in my accommodation he was likely to think I wouldn't be going anywhere until morning. It could quite possibly have been the case that no one was watching me and I had just been left to do my job, maybe I could have just strolled into the Marriot and picked up my passports and tickets and gone and jumped a flight straight back to England. This wasn't a chance I was willing to take though, I would only need to have my collar felt once and there was a very good chance I would never see daylight again.

I made my appearance look as much like that of a backpacker as I could and headed off for the train station. All the photo equipment stayed behind and my small pack contained only the bare essentials. I managed to secure a ticket on the Khyber mail train with the limited amount of cash I had on me. This left Peshawar for Lahore at 2240 hrs. Lahore was not too far from the Indian border and if I could get out of the country as soon as possible I would feel much better about the remainder of the journey back to Britain, even if I had no clue yet of the route it would take. The time was a little after ten which meant I had forty minutes of watching my back. I made my way to my platform and sat there on the bench with my pack on my knee trying to look as least like a hired killer as I could. I admit there was a small amount of panic welling in my stomach. Doing something like this and running away from a job could bring me nothing but trouble. I had never done it and didn't know what the result would be but I could only imagine it to be the ultimate punishment. The CIA cant have there freelance Field Ops walking out on jobs because they decided they didn't want to do it. I knew this was the end. Not only would I not get another paying job off them but they would more than likely now spend a few bob on having me removed from the picture. Mike would probably get a bollocking too for handing over shitty tools; the only thing good that could come of this was me keeping my ever-growing conscience in tact. I knew that the sister-in-law would more than likely be taken out by my replacement; this was beyond my control now. I wasn't here as a saviour or hero I just didn't want it to be me who did the deed. I had enough faces in my dreams I didn't need hers too. The most important thing now was getting home and sorting out my disappearance from the system.

The train was uncomfortable and overcrowded despite the time of night. After a few stops I managed to get myself a window seat and as nice a chap as I am there was no way I was getting up for anyone no matter how old or disabled they were. I put my pack behind my legs and tied it to them with the shoulder strap in case I somehow dosed off. All I could see in the glass of the window was the reflection of back inside the train, nothing much to look at for the next nine hours. I rested my forehead up against the cool glass and closed my eyes to try and streamline my extraction plan. I had no weapons limited funds and no clue of route restrictions or timings. I didn't know how long it was going to take me to get to safety or whether I would *be* safe when I got there. The next few days were certainly going to test me.

CHAPTER 15

I arrived in Lahore at eight thirty the following morning with the world's stiffest neck. When I got off the train I soon noticed the type of day it was going to be. It had only just gone half past eight in the morning but the warm Asian sun had already been up and out for three hours. I looked up at it to survey the sky for any possibility of relief from an occasional cloud but there was to be no such luck. When I brought my gaze back down to the peak hour street I had a huge purple dot bang in the centre of my vision along with a cluster of sweat beads across my forehead. There is a time and a place for a nice spot of sunshine but Lahore on a busy Saturday morning when your on the run from the CIA isn't one of them.

The dispute over Kashmir in the year 2000 was like a volcano ready to erupt. August 8th had seen the end of a fifteen day ceasefire when Hizbul Mujahideen revoked it. Talks had started on August 3rd between the Hizbul group and the Indian regime but when the Indian Prime

Minister Atal Bihari Vajpayee had refused to involve Pakistan in the discussions, Hizbul showed their upset by claiming fourteen lives with a car bomb blast in Srinagar. The year 2000 was not a good year to be trying to smuggle myself across the India Pakistan border.

I decided to take the risk and try my chances with the border guard. I didn't need to worry that they would be looking for me, I would only have been officially missing a couple of hours now and I would be surprised if the guys at the Embassy had already decided to admit they had lost me. I did however, need to worry that they simply wouldn't let me through because I was of Western origin or because I didn't have the correct papers so I had to get my story straight. Playing the dumb backpacking tourist was my best bet. I could show them my passport and permit to roam, which luckily had nothing on it about my being a photographer. If it did then it was in the bottom half that had been rendered illegible by days of sweat and creases. If it went off the colour of the paper I was just going to play dumb and hope for the best. To back myself up I withdrew a shit load of rupees from the ATM. This meant leaving an electronic footprint but I was confidant they had no details of my bank account. All that was left was to get to the crossing point and to hope that the official on duty today was either highly unprofessional or financially inconvenienced.

I took the bus from the stand on Badami Bagh along the thirty kilometres of the Grand Trunk Road to the border town of Wagha. On arrival there were forms and officials to negotiate for the next three hours. My travel documents and health certificates were all in order and all that was left for me to do was fill in the blanks and answer whatever questions the officials asked me with the best lies I had ever told. Everything was normal and I was passing through the system like everyone else. The only thing I had to worry about was the time it was taking. Every minute that passed brought me that much closer to being caught. This was the only border crossing point and as soon as I was reported missing this would be one of the first places they would call. The only thing that would stop them calling was not having a story in place for me. Calling Wagha and saying they had a rouge contract killer on the loose was not an easy option for them to take as it would involve too much explaining after I was caught.

I trickled slowly through the crossing procedure and was soon allowed out of Pakistan. I walked the five or six hundred meters through No Mans land to the Indian gateway at Attari where I caught a bus to the town of Amritsar. I almost felt as though I could relax but the forms I had filled out contained the details of an alias the company knew about, so they would know I was in India. I had no choice in using this as I had no time or means to change the details on my permit to those of my one remaining 'emergency passport'. If you didn't already know India is massive and as long as I had acquired forms which contained details from my one remaining passport by the time I reached Bangalore I would have effectively disappeared in somewhere in this wonderfully intricate country.

At Amritsar buying a train ticket without leaving any breadcrumbs proved more difficult than getting out of Pakistan. To buy tickets with cash the ticket office requires an exchange certificate an ATM receipt and a bankers card. Luckily I didn't find this out at the window so I was allowed some time to think up a valid story to avoid handing over anything that was going to give away my plans. Remember I still wasn't one hundred percent that the company didn't have my bank details and if the ticket office wanted to cross reference my card with my passport then I was certainly going to come unstuck.

At the window I managed to convince the girl that I had lost all my bank cards and official papers and desperately needed to get a train to Delhi so I could sort things out at my Embassy. It couldn't have been easier, the whole ATM receipt and bank cards is just a formality that can be easily overlooked with some good manners and a pleasant smile. The next obstacle was actually buying the ticket. Unfortunately for me you cannot just walk up to a ticket office in Amritsar and buy a ticket on the next train. The whole rail system there is so busy that all journeys need to be booked in advance. There is a very fair procedure in force there that means those who have planned their journey before hand can turn up knowing they won't have to struggle to find a seat. Those that need to travel at short notice can sign up for a reservation against cancellation which is self explanatory. This was my only option and since the girl I was now dealing with had already agreed to sell me a ticket without the required documentation I wasn't going to risk coming back later and being told that I couldn't travel. I put my name down and paid while I could. I was given a credit note to redeem for my ticket when there was a seat available for me. Once again I played the waiting game.

All this waiting around at stations and checkpoints was much like being on Sanger duty in Northern Ireland. Long boring shifts that seem to be never ending, wondering and in a strange way hoping for something to happen. If anything did happen I'd be fucked, but every now and then the boredom would briefly cause me to wish for someone to raise the alarm so I could spring into action. This irresponsible level of thought would only last for a millisecond before I would come to my senses again and be glad of the monotony. I'd find a seat on a hard bench and go through every possible seating position before I had to get up and walk around to maintain the blood flow in my legs. Doing this would cause me to lose my seat and I'd go through the whole cycle again over and over. When I did find brief moments of comfort I managed to build pictures in my tormented mind of the Albert Dock Williamson Square and the Jolly Miller at West Derby. I thought of Lauren and how her and Mike must be enjoying days out and nights in. I went over and over how I should have just quit when I was given the chance. I blamed greed for my decision to carry on, I tried to cover it up by telling myself that I did it to be financially sound should Mike or Lauren ever need me to be, but deep down I knew that Mike had more money set aside for their future than I could ever hope to amass in the time I had set myself. I was just feeling sorry for myself and clawing at any excuse I could to justify my stupid mistake.

If I though happy thoughts for too long then soon enough bad ones would creep in. It was if my own mind knew I wasn't entitled to anything good for too long a time because of what I had done over the last few years. My mind had become a twisted wreck of violence and mayhem and anything nice that was caught up in there was like an innocent passenger in a car accident that wasn't their fault.

The only chance I had at maintaining my sanity was to forget Lauren and Mike forget Liverpool and concentrate on the job and getting out of this place alive.

Once I had my travel documents sorted for my new passport it would be viable to assume I could travel from anywhere in India back to Britain. To get the blag forms though I had to approach the bad men in Delhi and occasionally the underworld in places like this has close links with representatives of my former employers. It wasn't always the case but there was a chance and chance favours the prepared mind.

At nine o'clock that night after eight hours of waiting in Amritsar station I was given a seat on the 21:30 to Delhi. The journey was to take around five hours and the seating arrangement was that of a small seating area with a fold down bunk hidden from other similar areas by a curtain each passenger could pull across to give them an element of privacy. I had been deprived of any comfort all day so with five hours to go I made the best of the most flat and softest surface I had come across since the accommodation at Peshawar.

The dim lighting made its way through the gaps around my curtain as I lay there listening to the conversations taking place in various languages along the train. The gentle sway of the train along with it rhythmic beat as the wheels passed over the sections of track somehow brought me peace. I thought nothing but pleasant thoughts for the duration of the journey and although I didn't sleep I rested well as the train made its way through the moonlit night to Delhi.

On a quiet day the streets of Delhi are like Fifth Avenue at 9am on a Monday morning. I had arrived at a little after 2am and after more waiting around I was able to sit and watch the city slowly come to life in almost orchestral timing to that of the sunrise. Delhi is a very clean and well kept city; unlike many other parts of India the platforms streets and parks are free from beggars. The parks contain picnicking families and people generally feel safer roaming the streets than they do in the smaller towns. Shopping centres have Western retail outlets like United Colours of Benetton and fast food places like MacDonald's and Wimpy. It is a very vibrant and colourful city and definitely worth a visit for recreational purposes. On Sundays the shops open early afternoon and close in the evening only to open again at night. Sunday nights in Delhi are like Friday nights in Liverpool, full of life. After another full day of killing time, walking the streets and taking in the sights it was night time again. I was past tired now, on my third or forth wind at least. Sleep would be of no use to me now, as long as I kept my blood sugar up my body would stay alert and awake. Darkness fell and I went searching for the hash dealers at the other side of town.

I didn't stand out too much, my clothes were seasoned from the long journey I had put them through and I had nothing of any value that would attract the local thieves to my presence. I wandered far beyond the main drag and turned on my Scally Radar, getting my hand signals ready in my mind to negotiate the deal I needed to acquire the blank tourist visa and health certificates for my onward journey.

The back streets of Delhi are like the most intricate maze you could ever imagine. With thin passageways and alleys that twist and turn enough to make you dizzy. Every doorway is selling something and most windows have a sign of some description above them. The power cables and phone lines overhead are literally as if someone as thrown a giant net over the city to keep its thousands of residents and visitors from falling off should the World stop spinning.

I strolled casually down the tight passageways making it known to the natives that I was walking without direction and wasn't in a rush to get anywhere. Some would look me up and down, others would smile as they passed me by and the occasional chancer would do his best to sell me something of little or no importance to the remainder of my journey. It wasn't long before I spotted what I could only assume to be a dodgy guy, if he wasn't selling drugs he was selling something he shouldn't. He was a scrawny young lad, leaning against the inside of an archway chewing the skin in between his fingers. Draped in his country's traditional dress of thin baggy pants and a long loose shirt he looked me up and down and through the gaps in his half eaten fingers raised his eyebrows in a suggestive manner. This could have meant a whole host of things of course, for all I knew he could have wanted to take me round the back and give me a rodgering for the rest of the night but I wasn't going to find out until I asked was I?

I made the universal hand signal for a ciggie and said "Smoke"? He gave me a "Yes" and smiled showing me a set of teeth that looked for the entire world like a row of bombed out terraced houses. I still didn't know if he meant he wanted one or had one for me and after I had established that I had to then upgrade the thing to a joint. Smoking weed in India is virtually legal, not officially but the police there will seldom follow up any hashish related incidents. The best way to get it is to hang around the 'Big Circle' and get on the back of a scooter which will take you where you need to go. Pot dealers here can be anyone and you don't have to be big and bad to sell it. I could have been traipsing from dealer to dealer all night trying to find my man which I why I steered clear of the tourist method and went looking for myself.

Being able to tell when someone is up to no good is a gift that I think all Scousers have. We seem to have acquired a name for ourselves over the years as a rum bunch who will rob you blind given half the chance. I think that is probably an unfair assessment of most of us, though I think those of us who are on the straight and level are still able to spot when someone is trying to pull the wool or when there is more to a person than first meets the eye. If all this lad did for a living was sell hash then why wasn't he out and about marketing it properly to the buyers up town? If he did sell the stuff then he had someone out peddling it for him while he stayed at home cultivating it and bagging up, that was my guess any how and after being invited in to his dark and dusty living room it was only a matter of minutes before I was proved correct.

"You like smoke the hashish?" He said in broken English.

"Sure!" I replied. "How much?" Rubbing my fingers and thumb together. I didn't have a clue how much it was supposed to cost but it worked out about a tenner for a shit load so I wasn't complaining. We sat on his battered cane furniture looking out into the dusty passageway outside and smoked his gear through a water cooled pipe. I gave him more money than he had asked for and at the same time took out my documents to make my original request. It took a good few minutes of pointing to the document and asking over and over in the simplest possible English I could find. It must be so annoying for foreigners on the receiving end of an Englishman who thinks if he talks slowly to them like they are idiots there is no reason why he shouldn't be understood. This isn't the case with me as I'm not as arrogant as some people and I totally sympathise with them. Never the less I began to speak to him slowly and had to put my hand on his shoulder and apologise for the hint of unintentional arrogance he must have sensed. I endeavoured though and it wasn't long before he began to understand what I was saying.

We battled on for the next half an hour, I not speaking any Hindi and my new friend not speaking much English. He was doing better than me though and I couldn't help but respect him for his effort to try and learn our language. The terms were soon agreed and the only part that troubled me was having to wait two days. I suspected he wanted to be a middle man in the deal rather than just pass me on to those who could help me. I wasn't concerned with this as whatever he was going to charge me I could afford and there was no way I was that unlucky that I had just walked into the living room of a company asset. He wanted me to pay half up front and come back

162

in two days, there was no way this was going to happen and we ended up agreeing on ten percent. The wait was what concerned me, what the hell was I going to do in Delhi for two days? I didn't have a clue how close behind me the company was, if at all they were but I couldn't really afford to take the risk. There wasn't much choice in the matter though so it was just something I had to deal with. I left him with his money and made my way back to the safety of the main streets. For all I knew I had just been robbed but what could I do? I was in his pond now and I just had to sit tight and hope.

I got a room in the Connaught which at most was a couple of kilometres from the train station, which I had opted to be my exit point. It was late and after a great cup of tea in Tiffany's I retired to my room. I peeled off my clothes and washed them in the bath tub with the complimentary shower gel before scrubbing myself back to an acceptable level of cleanliness. Razors and foam toothpaste and deodorant were all included in the fancy little basket in the bathroom. My personal hygiene had suffered terribly over the last few days and although I did what I could to stay on top of it, it wasn't long before the heat of the sun and the constant moving around saw to it that I was back to square one. I had been chewing wood to keep my teeth clean and in true Infantry fashion the only part of my body to be maintained correctly was my feet. Now was the perfect opportunity to clean up and after the shave and cleaning my teeth several times I felt normal again. The only thing left now was to catch up on some sleep. I didn't have to be anywhere any time soon so after securing the door and removing the coat hanging rail from my wardrobe for defence purposes I turned out the lights and climbed into the spotlessly clean white sheets. After a huge sigh I closed my eyes and contently smiled to myself. I had got this far without any major problems so if nothing else I deserved this night's sleep to be free from bad thoughts. It was 2am and the streets outside were getting quieter by the minute. I drifted off into the abyss of sleep wondering what the dreams had in store for me this time.

CHAPTER 16

I slept right through to 7am totally undisturbed. No bad dreams and no unwelcome visitors just five full hours of blissful sleep. I felt totally recharged and ready to face the day, whatever it had to throw at me. I hadn't felt this confidant for days; I was back to my usual self again. Confidant, almost cocky but most of all not fearful or phased by the fact I had the CIA somewhere behind me. The best way I thought I could shake them off would be to zigzag across the country to my exit route of Bangalore. Bangalore as the crow flies was eleven hundred miles away. I had no idea, if any how many miles behind me they were. I had to assume at all times that they weren't too far and employ evasion drills every step of the way. I only needed to be caught up with once and it was pretty much over for me. It wouldn't be a case of fighting my way to freedom I would be taken out from a distance and left to bake in the August sun until the Indian police decided to turn up and move my body.

I ate a light breakfast so as not to stretch my stomach, my food intake over the last few days had been minimal, mostly fast burning sugars. I didn't know when I was going to be eating again, and with a stretched stomach you become hungrier quicker. Some cakes and jam and a gallon of coffee was all it took to set me up. I filled in some pages of my personal journal as I had done since training and caught a bus further into town. After a stroll around the market I decided to buy some clothes that would help me blend in a bit more. I'm all English but I was blessed with thick black hair and dark skin and after I geared up like the natives there was no telling me apart until you asked me to speak.

The following night at 8pm I made my way back to Hash boy's place hoping that I hadn't been ripped off. If I had then I had to do the whole thing again and probably wait another two days. As I approached sure enough he was stood in the exact position he had been two nights previous. He smiled and called out "Hello English!" I took this as a good sign, had he not have had my forms surely he would have at least attempted to avoid me. He invited me in but this time I declined. Who knew what traps had been set up in the last forty eight hours, whatever requests he made I had to avoid granting him. If any traps had been set then I would only be making it easier for them if I danced to their tune. "Everything good?" I asked him.

"Good! Yes." he replied.

He went back inside to retrieve my stuff. It turned out to be all innocent and good natured but I couldn't help but be on edge. The forms were top notch and I couldn't be sure whether he knew someone who could get real ones or had copies made. All the boxes were blank ready for me to fill in and the stamp which usually ends up over the writing was slightly off to one side. We exchanged smiles and I gave him his money. He attempted once again to get me inside for a smoke but it wasn't happening and soon after I left him chewing his hand again in the comfort of his doorway.

Luckily the train I needed was leaving at 21:15 and after my last experience I decided to use the free time I had had to book my ticket in advance. The Indian rail network is the second largest of its kind in the world, only Russia's is bigger. Over 14,000 trains carry 12,000,000 passengers daily and booking your ticket in advance is really the only answer to a smooth and comfortable journey.

When the train pulled into the station the people on the platform stampeded onto the carriages while the porters pushed the luggage on anywhere they could, including through the windows. I couldn't understand what all the rushing was about as everyone getting on must have had a reserved seat or compartment. I stood shaking my head at the organised chaos and casually made my way to my air conditioned sleeper. At the ticket office I attempted to purchase a ticket for a single berth sleeper unfortunately there were non and since there was no way I was sharing with a snoring stranger for the next three days I had to pay for the two seats. The extra room was great though, two reclining seats gave somewhere to sit during the day whilst two drop down bunks were at hand for the night. The first fifteen minutes of my journey was spent securing the lock on my compartment door. Although it worked my Nan could have kicked the thing open and she's been dead for fifteen years.

The route I was taking took about 38 hours and had more stops than I could count so again my patience was going to be tested. It was a case of sitting back and taking in the sights for the next few days. Right now though it was getting on for 10pm and after another hot tiring day of wandering aimlessly I decided to make the most of the free time. I locked up my berth and wandered the length of the train looking for any faces that didn't fit the environment. After satisfying myself that none of them had made it onto the train I retired back to my cabin passing a waiter on the way and ordering some tea and butties. The food was awful but I ate it just the same, the tea however was quite reasonable and after drinking it and washing up I lay back on my bunk to give some thought to streamlining my extraction plan.

This train was bound for Madras where I would change to make my way across to Bangalore. Apparently there are three different gauges of track through out the Indian rail network and because of this one has to change on occasion to navigate the country. To be honest I didn't know where I had to change or why. I had attempted to plan my route down to the smallest detail but when I gave thought to the abundance of unforeseen circumstances that could alter my plans along the way I decided to just take trips in the general direction of my target destination. My rail map showed me the routes I needed to take to get to Bangalore and that was enough for me. The more uncertainty I applied to the plan the harder I would be to track. It wasn't a case of being poorly prepared or not putting enough effort into my strategy. I couldn't be sure of anything and the amount of contingencies that would have to be in force were unrealistic so the route itself was at the bottom of my priority list. Instead I focused on my immediate position, making sure I didn't place myself in situation s I would find it difficult to get out of, preparing emergency exit routes from my cabin and being overly curious of everyone I came into contact with. Getting to where I was going, although important was lower down on my list of priorities than getting there alive. I didn't care how long it took or how many times I had to travel up and down this country or the next, I had to get back to West Derby alive and without a tail.

By the time I arrived in Madras I felt as though I had turned the corner. My wheel was still spinning but the hamster was well and truly dead. I was almost stir crazy. I could only imagine what it must be like to be sentenced to life imprisonment and spend the rest of your days in such a small cell. Two and a half days on that train was more than enough for me to promise myself that if I was ever captured and sentenced to a facility where escape was impossible then I would process myself at my earliest possible convenience. To think that some people actually do that for a holiday, sit on a train for all that time. Amazing. I won't take anything away from India itself, the scenery and culture would truly be a delight to experience but certainly not from a 6 x 6 'cell'. If it hadn't have been for the fact that I had the compartment to myself and the air conditioning was on the ball I would have got off and walked at Faridabad.

After another wait at Madras I was soon on route to Bangalore, my final stop before I felt it safe to board a plane. Six or seven hours later I had arrived and I found the difference between the South and North of India to be quite considerable. Everything here seemed so much slower and less important than the North. The temperate climate is much milder due to the city's elevation and as a result it stays pretty much pleasant all year round. Peak hour traffic flowed much easier than that of Delhi and even the people seemed more relaxed. This and the fact that I was feeling much safer now I had travelled so far without a hint of trouble, led to me being much more comfortable with my circumstances. People leave their jobs everyday because they aren't happy with the demands put on them. Why should the CIA be any different? If they weren't happy with me leaving the way I did then that's their problem not mine. If they come after me then they better send their best because I'm ready for them. No this wasn't me being too big for my boots. In the past few years I had got away with murder in a whole host of different circumstances. I had taken my conventional combat skills of the Regular Army and combined them with those of the Intelligence Corps. After some hands on experience I felt as though I was pretty good at taking lives and clandestinely withdrawing from the area. I had never once been close to being caught and as a result my confidence was high.

From Bangalore I flew to Bandaranaike International Airport in Sri Lanka and after a few more lies at customs and handing over more departure taxes I managed to get a flight into Heathrow. This is were the passport desks would light up if they were going to. On the flight into London I thought non stop about ways to explain myself if anything hit the fan when I handed over my passport. Before 9/11 machine readable passports were not a necessity so the battered old American one I had would not raise any alarms on the computer system. I had acquired it from Mike when I worked for him and I was unsure what procedures he had to follow to get me it. Where the details logged on another system somewhere? Did the passport control official have the details of it? Or had the Intelligence divisions that once employed me to sit behind that desk appointed someone to look for me in particular? The only way I was going to find out now was to just go for it. I was 38,000ft over the Indian Ocean; I couldn't exactly turn back now.

When I arrived I was asked questions like; how did I get into Sri Lanka? How long had I been gone? What had been my business? By now I looked well and truly like a student. My hair had grown out of control I was unshaven and I was still wearing the traditional Indian dress I had bought in Delhi so after looking me up and down a few times I was waved through. Back then getting in and out of a country illegally was easier than buying fish in Grimsby, very sad I suppose that it should take something as tragic as 9/11 to put an end to it.

I wasn't going to push my luck with airport security so I opted again for the train back up to Liverpool. Now I was back in Mainland Britain I felt safe about calling home. I had it in my head that if the company was monitoring any telephone networks they would be looking for calls to England originating in Pakistan or India, as you can imagine this would already total thousands daily so even in the remote instance that they were monitoring these calls they certainly wouldn't be bothering with mainland calls. I know now that this was all just paranoia but it was healthy paranoia as I don't believe a person can be too cautious. During training in Quantico I was lectured on how sophisticated and effective telephone monitoring within the various Government departments was but I was also briefed on how expensive it was to operate. I really couldn't see them employing the system to find one runaway freelance field op.

If they had my home address details then this put a whole different spin on things. My address would give them my phone number, and my phone number something to focus their attention on. I couldn't see how they could find this out though. The house in West derby had been bought through a limited company that had no traceable link to the limited company I was paid through for my work. I had a nominee service which would take money from my business account, split it into smaller amounts and deposit it into accounts that I could use without fear of being traced. Since the transaction was not electronic and the amounts deposited were different to the amounts withdrawn the paper trail ended with the nominee service, which I paid through the teeth for annually.

After changing some money I made my way to the phone box to ring Mike. I dialled the area code 0..1..5..1.... As my finger dialled the forth digit my heart sank. I hung up the phone and looked quickly for somewhere to sit. I felt instantly cold and sick. How could I have been so stupid? Panic hit me like a cricket bat across the back of my head. Where had I gone wrong to slip up like I did? How could I get so far thinking I was unstoppable and miss such a simple detail?

I had three company accounts in total. The first is the one I used to invoice the company for, my fees would be paid into this. Every quarter a sum would be withdrawn and after my instalment for the service had been removed the remaining amount would be split between two accounts which I had named 'Existing' and 'Living'. 'Existing' being the account that paid all bills to do with the house car etc and 'Living' for day to day expenditure. The deposits for both these accounts were made in the same building which meant with a bit of research and some common sense if you found one you could find a link to the other. The ATM at Lahore. I was so mad at myself, if this is where they tracked me then all the train journeys and zigzagging was for nothing. I felt physically sick. I thought I was being smart by not using my business account which could pin point my position. Why didn't I give it more thought? If they monitored all ATM transactions from the border areas then found a link between one and a house in Liverpool it couldn't be easier for them.

Shit! I had to phone home anyway to warn Mike and Lauren, but it had been over a week now. If anyone had been going to call they would have done it by now. The line rang out over and over. When it cut off I tried again, several times. There were so many possibilities where Mike could be; in town in Washington or dead.

I had to formulate some kind of a plan and as fast as possible. Mike could just be out for the day, in which case I could sit off and keep trying up until what I considered to be a reasonable time for them to have returned. He and Lauren could be away for a few days in which case I would have to make the trip up to Liverpool to confirm everything was still ok. There was also the possibility that both he and Lauren were lying there dead, I didn't have a solution for this.

I had to take the chance; this was Mike and Lauren we were talking about here. If the company had traced me back to the house Mike and Lauren would either be already dead in trouble or on the run. I couldn't bear to think of them like that especially knowing it was my fault for being so stupid. I took the express into London then transferred to a connection for Liverpool. I spent the next few hours hoping they were both ok and knowing that should they not be I would blame myself for the rest of my life.

Unlike the train to Scotland this one couldn't move fast enough. I just wanted it to be back in Liverpool, yesterday. All I could think about was Lauren being harmed and Mike trying in vain to help her. Both of them being executed in cold blood and left for the rats in the cold wet gutter of some shitty street. My head was upside down I'd have given my whole world for them to be safe. Tucked up in my house in West Derby with no one but us knowing their whereabouts. What had I done?

The train arrived in Lime Street at 20:50 and after a tormenting taxi ride to the bottom of the road I threw a tenner at the driver and approached the house in the best way I knew how.

A hundred or so meters from the house I could break track and head for the end of the back garden. I disappeared into the trees and bushes and found myself a decent sized half Charlie. I climbed the fence to the rear of the house and crept up to the back kitchen door. The house was dark and the security lights made a noticeable impression on the lawn as they illuminated it on my approach. The house appeared deserted but I needed to be sure. I took the key from underneath the flagstone to the right of the kitchen door. I prayed the alarm was on. If it was it meant if anyone was inside the house then they had been stood still for an eternity as the motion sensors would not allow any object to travel faster than 0.5 mph past them. As the door opened the sensors picked up my movement and triggered the delay. I had thirty seconds to get to the panel and enter the access code. Still weary that someone was there waiting for me I moved quickly yet cautiously through the darkness with the brick in my hand raised and ready to strike. If anyone was here then they knew of my presence by now so turning on the lights would not matter. As I entered the hall way I flicked on every light switch I passed until I reached the panel and entered the code, first five digits of my Army number. The panel beeped three times indicating that the system was disarmed. I made my way upstairs clearing every room I passed with nothing but half a house brick. As I got to the first bedroom I accessed the safe behind the door and took out the loaded .38 that I had bought for three hundred pound from a bloke in Salford not long after the three of us had arrived back from Washington. I pulled back the hammer to minimise the trigger travel should I need to get a round off rapidly. I made my way around the house clearing every possible hiding place for would be assassins. Nothing! After a good half hour of being convinced I wasn't alone in my huge house I came to the conclusion that I was. Back in the living room there was a plate with two slices of margarita pizza on it lying in the middle of the couch. The tiny bite marks in it told me it had been Lauren's. Clearly the two of them had left in a hurry as Lauren always finished her pizza. And Mike would always have cleared up after her. It was then I knew that they had made a run for it. There was no signs of a struggle which meant they had left of their own accord but they had certainly had no time to plan or pack. The sink was full of dishes and the kitchen bin was full. Mike would never have left the place like this, he was far too meticulous.

I didn't know what to do next. With everything that had gone on I couldn't even calm myself enough to think straight. The two of them could be anywhere and if Mike hadn't left a note its because he knew someone other than myself would find it. After securing the house again I sat in the bedroom and explored my options. I went over and over every possibility in my head but when I attempted to give myself an answer I couldn't. Truth is they could be anywhere and if I hadn't been left a message then I would never find them. I knew that deep down Mike wouldn't just let me sweat it out; he would be in touch soon to let me know how to catch up with them. Right now I had to stay calm and be ready for any unwanted guests. I sat in the bedroom furthest away from the stairs with my .38 and waited out the night in the armchair. In the morning I would start the search, right now I had to make it through the night. I knew I couldn't sleep but I had to at least try.

CHAPTER 17

In the morning I awoke startled with the noise of my neighbour across the street putting out his bin. I shot up to look out the window and standing well back noticed him looking at the house with a curious expression on his face. I wanted to go out and ask him if he had seen anyone suspicious or even if he knew where Mike and Lauren where, but the less people that knew anything was wrong the better. I wandered around the house with the .38 in my hand not knowing where to start. The only other place I could think of was the house in Washington but he wouldn't go there, not into the lions den.

I ate a tin of cold beans and sausages and drinking from a bottle of water I watched Sky news to catch up on the goings on in the Western World. My eyes and ears absorbed the information and sent it back to the brain for processing. What happened when it got there I don't know, I never was any good at biology. What I do know is that whatever I was watching that day on sky news was lost in my synapses as I battled to find answers to what had happened in my life and how I was going to fix it. I longed to retire and get on the waiting list for my season ticket, make some drinking friends in the local and get caught staring down the bar maid's top occasionally. Maybe even take her home and leave the life of cold blooded murder far behind me as I learnt how to be a boyfriend. I found myself praying. To who I don't know, I was never a believer in God but I wanted someone to be there so badly. Someone who could tell me that I was forgiven and everything was going to be ok. After the brief spell of feeling sorry for myself I snapped back to the real world. People needed saving and more people had to die for this to happen. Think!

The most prominent thought in my mind was that whoever had chased Mike away would soon be back for me. I set the scene in my mind of managing to incapacitate and interrogate them to find out some sort of lead. It never happens like this though. It's almost always a case of fighting for survival and one of you always ends up dead. I hoped for the situation to arise all the same.

Around 10am, after a cup of Rosie, I went to drop the kids off at the pool. After sitting there for several minutes I reached for the toilet paper. As I pulled off a strip a ten pence coin fell out of the roll and hit the tiled floor. I watched curiously as it rolled towards the bath. My first thought was booby trap, on clearing the house I hadn't thought of this one. I had checked all doors and drawers cupboards and chairs, but the fuckin' Gary Glitter? What kind of sick twat rigs the Gary? I cringed as I waited for the blast, it felt like a life time. I thought about how thousands of tiny pieces of porcelain where about to pepper my insides, but nothing came. Instead the coin had been put there to draw my attention to the section of toilet roll I was now holding. On it in blue biro was some writing. "Ormond Beach Golf Club". I knew it was from Mike but where the hell was Ormond Beach?

Mike's little coin trick, as you would expect, made my trip to the toilet a lot easier than it had to be so I immediately set to trying to find his safe house. After a short spell on the Internet I found it near Daytona in Florida. I was expecting it to be in Newquay or something to be honest. The last thing I felt like was another nine hour flight so soon after the last but never the less I didn't think twice and after shaving and washing my hair I changed into some jeans a sweat top and my Rockport's.

My journal, which usually travelled everywhere with me was stashed in the attic. Anything could happen this time and the last thing I wanted was a written confession to all my jobs ending up in the wrong hands. I took a wad of cash and my British passport out of the safe and headed for Manchester. Again I had to wait right through until 8:30 the next morning for a flight, that combined with the nine hour journey in economy class meant that when I arrived at Orlando International Airport my personal hygiene was once again in the red. During the flight over I sat next to an extremely talkative young lad who despite my efforts to ignore him managed eventually to squeeze a conversation out of me. As it turned out he was an English student pilot travelling to Embry-Riddle Aeronautical University in Daytona. At first I though I may be able to bum a lift off him but it turned out his University bus was picking him up and I wasn't invited. The conversation with him wasn't totally meaningless though. He advised that I should get in touch with some of the flight schools when I arrive and ask if anyone is doing a full stop landing at Orlando and wants to have half their time paid for by taking me back to Ormond. Apparently there is a small municipal airport there a stones throw from the golf course. Quite amazing I thought that I could go from my front door to seeing Mike and Lauren on the other side of the World by using only three vehicles.

Sure enough the kids plan worked and within sixty minutes of disembarking the 747 I was squeezing myself into a Cessna with some spotty kid. He had only be given his license two months previous and as he fired us down the runway in his winged go-cart I couldn't help but wonder if a hire car would have been the better option. I watched the needles on the dials bouncing all over the place and the ground start to slip away from under us. Although I wasn't able to hear myself think the thoughts came all the same and I had now resigned myself to the fact that if I was here in Florida to die then putting myself in situations like this was only going to speed up the process. The kid doing the flying thought the whole thing was great, I don't think he stopped smiling once. I must admit I could feel the buzz myself but I had responsibilities to take care of before I fell 3000ft from the sky in a plastic plane.

After bouncing 30ft the first time and 10ft the second we managed to get the thing down on the runway at Ormond. Whilst taxiing back to his parking place I thanked him and gave him a handful of dollars which he was more than happy with. As I walked off I felt a slight twinge of envy. I wished I could be his age again and maybe have been sent out here by my rich parents to learn to fly planes in the gorgeous Florida sun. I longed to have my time over. Go to college, get a great job and travel the world being a normal person instead of being in all this trouble. I had enough money to move out here if I wanted and do this everyday. In fact when I found Mike and Lauren I was going to propose this to them. If Mike could maybe find a way to get us out of this mess then why not? The place was gorgeous and I couldn't think of anything better. Mike had been respected by all those above him in his time, he had served them well and I reckon they must have owed him the odd favour. I bet he had already thought of a plan to free the three of us from this vicious circle.

At the Golf club I told the guy I was looking for a friend who had arranged to meet me here.

"What's your friend's name"? He asked.

"His name is Mike he has a young girl with him called Lauren, his daughter." I replied.

"Oh yes, that would make you Uncle Mally right"? I wasn't sure whether it was a statement or a question but I said "Yes" anyway.

"He left a phone number for you; you can use this phone here." He pointed to his desk then walked out the room.

I wasted no time and rang the number. Mike answered.

"Mike, what the hell is going on"? I shouted, not angrily but certainly with a hint of stress in my tone of voice.

"Fuckin' hell mate, thank God for that. I'll be there in five minutes." He hung up.

No more than five minutes later a black Chrysler pulled onto the car park and I turned my attention from the spotty kid tying his plane to the floor to Mikes smiling face at the window. In a comical but agitated way I told him what I had been through to get here and how I was nearly processed by the hands of a seventeen year old pilot. We sat there in the Chrysler for a few moments and talked about how we should move here, if we can just put this ugly mess behind us. I told him how lost I had felt when I didn't know where to look or if anything had happened to him and Lauren. He made his apologies then told me how we had to think fast as Keiron was at the house we were going to.

"Are you having a laugh"? I said.

"No, they came to West Derby to wait for you, I didn't know who they were or what they wanted at the time so I took Lauren and ran here. I've got an old friend who has a house round the corner."

"What is he here for? Have they come to take me down? Is he alone?" I interrupted.

"Mally, calm down. Listen to yourself." Mike said.

I admit I must have sounded like a scared kid but I just wanted as many questions answering as I could before we got to the house.

"Originally they came to West Derby to turn you off, simply because that's the easy option, you know the score. I've spoke to him now though and he just wants to here your reasons and be given a full debriefing then I reckon he will just move on. He's a reasonable bloke." He said with a smile.

"Yeah right! None of them are reasonable. If he is alone I will half believe it. How long has he been here?" I asked.

"He has been here three days, we didn't know when to expect you back and yes he is alone, unless his backup has been sleeping in his car for the last 72 hours." Mike always had to try and put humour into everything.

"We have to plan for every eventuality though mate so put this in your pocket." He handed me a Glock.

"So you haven't really got a clue whether he is reasonable or not have you?" I said.

"Better safe than dead mate." He replied.

At the house Mike entered first. On the way up the drive I had made a mental note of every detail. My one true gift working over time. Trying to assess every possible escape route should something go terribly wrong. I really couldn't see how they were just going to let me off with this. I convinced myself that if there were only three people in this house then there would only be two coming out alive. As I passed over the threshold I put my hand on Mike's shoulder.

"Where's Lauren?"

"Somewhere safe until we are mate, don't worry." He replied.

As I entered the lounge Keiron jumped up form his chair, my hand flinched around the gun in my pocket.

"Jesus Christ Mally this better be the best fuckin' story I ever heard." He cried.

Is it wrong to pick a Rose within its prime?

To exploit what it gives for the rest of its time.

In a single reap its life will end.

But past its peak, too late to mend?

The best of its last or the last of its best.

Either way it's losing the last of its zest.

Make the most of its passion and allow it to shine.

Let it do what it does best for the rest of its time.

He won't have even seen it coming, which after the years of service he had given the game, was probably the least he deserved. The bullet took the back of his head off before he even heard the quiet clink of the firing mechanism. I know what we did in that room was wrong. The guy we had just killed had been on the same team over the years and had really only wanted the same as the rest of us; to contribute to making the World a safer place. Who ultimately decides if we made the right choices or not I suppose will one day make themselves known to us. For the time being though I guess I'll just have to hope we all got it right, if at all it is ever right to take another life. In that room in Florida someone had to die to put an end to the story and as long as it wasn't Lauren or her Dad then I could live with that.

Since I pulled the trigger I got straight out of there and went to see Lauren who was in a house at the end of the estate with the wife and family of the 'old friend'. The only other man in her life that could keep her safe stayed to clean up the body. When everything was cleaned and the whole thing wrapped up we said our goodbyes and headed back to Liverpool, maybe one day I'll move out to Florida but right now I quite like Liverpool and Lauren wanted to start school there.

It was mid September 2000 Lauren was eleven and ready for secondary school. She started at Holly Lodge girl's school and we lived together in the house in West Derby. Lauren managed to live the next couple of years free from the majority of life's cruelty, but I think this was warranted by the fact she had had more than her fair share over the years.

I would do anything to protect Lauren; I would murder or save who ever I had to, to keep her safe. Sometimes life is fair and you are blessed by an unknown force to have someone so special in your life. Other times life is unfair and you have special people taken away, like Hailey. I don't think there is a balance. I think some people have all the good and others have all the bad while the lucky ones have a bit of both. Most would say the lucky ones are the ones are those who have all the good but I disagree. If every day had nothing but good in it, would we appreciate it as much? I know when Hailey died I appreciated Lauren more.

After Hailey, Lauren was the only innocence in this story, everyone else was guilty of one thing or another. If someone less innocent had to die to keep her from harm then, how ever close they were to me, I wouldn't hesitate.

Like I said, one day I will be judged on my decisions to end lives but one thing I am sure of is, that no God or Celestial being will ever make me feel bad about decisions I made to keep Lauren safe. I made my choices and I'll stand by them and if God is pissed at me, well, he better send his best.

CHAPTER 18

From around chapter five I started to get the impression that this whole story was much too far fetched to be real, one thing I will say is that I did see the journal and for someone to fill it in like they had over the years would make this a pretty obsessive lie. I mean I'm just an average bloke, how would I end up writing the life story of a government assassin?

For the duration of my visits to the house in Liverpool I was told Mike and Lauren were both in Florida. If they were real people then I did not find any reason for this to be a lie. However, certain things did not ring true and as much as I wanted to believe a lot of the story I did struggle to. For one I could not understand why the CIA would not follow up Keiron's disappearance. If he was as high ranking as the story claimed then why would he not tell anyone where he was going, and how would he get to the rank he had without being smart enough to assume that Mike and Mally might just bump him off? It was a nice story and would probably make a good action film if someone wanted to buy the film rights but journal aside, I began to think the whole thing had been thought up in the bar of the Jolly Miller on a Sunday afternoon. One thing I will say about Malcolm Wilson is, if Mike and Lauren did exist then he thought the world of them and probably *would* have died for them. His knowledge of weapons and places around the globe either came from a lot of research or time in the forces, but an assassin? I couldn't be sure. It is not often I am fooled by a yarn spinner, something about them always seem to light them up as a liar. This time though it was so hard to tell.

I remembered his promise of telling me the truth after I delivered the finished product and after typing fifty odd thousand words out for him I took the printed pages down to the house in West Derby. It was not so much the rest of my money I was looking forward to now it was knowing the truth. I think the truth I wanted to hear was that he had made it all up so I could take my money and leave being thankful that I had not just made friends with a cold blooded killer.

I had not been to the house for a fortnight. I had been at my computer typing non stop for as long as I can remember. When I arrived something was not right. I moved up to the windows to find the inside mostly bare with nothing but several tea chests filling the halls.

I knew instantly that he had left and felt well and truly 'ripped off'. Not for the money or the time and effort that had gone unrecognized but for not being told whether I was holding a fifty thousand word lie or the biography of Liverpool's coldest killer.

I made my way around the house looking for some signs of hope that he would be returning but every door and window was locked. At the back kitchen door were several bags of junk and rubbish ready for the bins. A cat had made a top job of ripping open one of the bags and pulling all sorts of scraps of food out over the floor. He was long gone. Sticking out the bag was what looked to be the corner of a DVD player or games console. I was in the sort of mood where I wanted to take something of value away from the whole experience whatever form it took so after a quick look round I rummaged through the bags of junk. The DVD player turned out to be a snazzy cordless telephone and digital answering machine which I quickly stuffed down my coat before leaving and returning home.

Some days later, after reading my story again several times, I plugged in my swag to see if I could make any use of it. The casing was cracked but it worked just fine and it looked ok too once I wiped the egg yoke off it.

When it fired up properly it read as having two old messages, the first one was from Safestyle windows. The second one went something like this;

"Hi dad, listen I don't know what time you think our flight is but...." the message was interrupted by a voice which was clearly in the house at the time of the call.

"Hiya Lauren it's me, just a minute...." There was a beep and the message ended.

The hairs on the back of my neck stood up and my whole body turned to ice. I felt sick, dizzy, scared. The male voice in the call was that of the story teller but it was not the same as it had been the last few months. It was not Scouse any more, it was American. How could someone have spoken a hundred thousand words to me and I not spotted they were putting on the accent? It's hardly the easiest accent to fake and he even knew Scouse slang. Everything fell into place. My hand started shaking uncontrollably. I was instantly petrified. There were a few possibilities as to why he had done this. Was Mally an American all along? I doubted this, he knew too much about being brought up in Liverpool and what would be the point in lying about this? Had Mally even existed? Was it Mike I had been speaking to all this time? I know that the conclusion I came to is the one that I consider without doubt to be true. Every time I read through my notes and the story it becomes clearer. When I first realized I sat on the foot of my bed and sobbed for what seemed like an eternity. If this story is true and not just some very well researched lie, then it was Mally who had died in that room in Florida. The CIA did not come looking for Keiron because he was not missing. He was 'the only other person who could keep Lauren safe'. If Mike killed Mally for him then why would Keiron not let him and Lauren live in peace? Contractors die permanent staff retire. I thought about Mally, he left his journal here before leaving for Florida. Mike must have found it. Why has he done this? Why has he told his secrets to me? Mally's loyalty to them made me sob like a child. He loved them with all his heart and he paid for it with his life.

What pressure must Mike have been put under to do that to his best friend? I kept reading the last chapter over and over. Everything made sense now. I wonder if Mally had seen it coming? If in his final seconds he could press pause and stand back to see what was going on, would he understand? Would he forgive Mike? The only reason he would have done this was to keep Lauren safe? Mike knew he could not protect Lauren from an entire Government department so this was his only choice. I longed to know Malcolm so I could ask him for myself, then it dawned on me. I did know him. This was *his* story, told by his best friend. A best friend who now had to live wondering whether he had been forgiven for his decision to protect his only daughter and only living proof that his late wife ever existed by shooting his best friend in the back of the head.

I wanted Mally to be known for his loyalty to these two people who he loved more than life itself; however sad and lonely life was for him. Maybe deep down he knew it would never end unless the most powerful force in that room got what it wanted. I prayed he was somewhere better than where he had spent his living years. He may have been a killer but he had really convinced himself he was removing evil from the world by doing so. He was an excellent soldier, maybe the best of his class but he had been blinded by love and loyalty that sadly had never been returned to him. He was an infinite bank of knowledge when it came to the skills of a warrior but where the workings of the human mind and heart where concerned you could not find a person more naïve. He gave love and loyalty to a family that took him into their home and their hearts, but gave no thought to the priorities that Mike had to deal with that sunny day in Florida. I suppose if his beliefs were incorrect and there is an after life, he will find time there to learn to understand that life here on earth is a lot more complex than the black and white he had been taught. I know his love for Mike as a friend will allow him to forgive him and understand why he did what he did. I know in my heart that God will forgive him. He was taught to kill from too early an age to see that they were not his decisions to make and still his heart told him how to love. His conscience was taken away from him and by meeting Lauren and her family it fought its way back stopped him from killing again and freed him from the life he thought he would die living. On his journey back through India to Liverpool he was a free man.

Despite what he did with his life I know from what I have written that Malcolm Wilson had a good heart and I will think of him everyday, and pray he is somewhere nicer than here.

Is it wrong to pick a Rose within its prime?

To exploit what it gives for the rest of its time.

In a single reap its life will end.

But past its peak, too late to mend?

The best of its last or the last of its best.

Either way it's losing the last of its zest.

Make the most of its passion and allow it to shine.

Let it do what it does best for the rest of its time.

Mike...

ABOUT THE AUTHOR

Robbie O'Grady was born in Liverpool in 1976. Having left the City in his early teens Robbie spent some time living in Lancashire before joining the Infantry at the age of Seventeen.

Now out of the Army he has returned to Liverpool where he enjoys writing stories that combine his own experiences with those of others and input from his extremely creative imagination. Much of his work is unpublished but hopefully more of it will follow the example of 'A Sequence of Events' and become published paperbacks for all to enjoy.

Until now his love of writing has remained a secret to most of the people around him and was purely for personal creative pleasure. Now though the thought of sharing his work with others is very much appealing to Robbie and he hopes you enjoy reading it as much as he did writing it.

Printed in the United States
96711LV00001B/219/A